2036:
The Year Trump Stepped Down!
A Horrifying and Factual Account, Sent Back in Time (through Three Black Holes) to some Random, Hack Writer

(by Michael Sandels)

Please check out my other novels, all available on Amazon, Kindle, and stores:

The End of the Word as We Know It

artism

Extra Special Sauce

The Water Salesman

Two Thumbs Sticking Up!

How to Win Over and Screw Affluent People Through Crime (And Remain Sane)

And my children's book: "The Magical, Grown-Up ABC Phone Book"

Please send any questions to m.me/MSandels

or visit my Author's Pages: fb.me/MSandels or

http://www.amazon.com/author/michaelsandels

2036: The Year Trump Stepped Down by Michael Sandels

Table of Contents

Chapter One

Chapter Two

"December"
Loser-Sanctuary-Dirty Chicago December 9, 2036
Canadian Border December 11, 2036
The Saint-Louis White-Cardinal White-House December 25, 2036
The 4 Sticks December 26, 2036.
Cincinnati Proper December 27, 2036
Rapid City Gorge White House December 29, 2036

Chapter Three

Cincinnati Tuesday, December 31, 2036
Hamilton, Ohio Sticks December 31, 2036
2 miles beneath the Washington DC White House
December 31, 2036
Cincinnati December 31, 2036
The After-Math

For Jordan

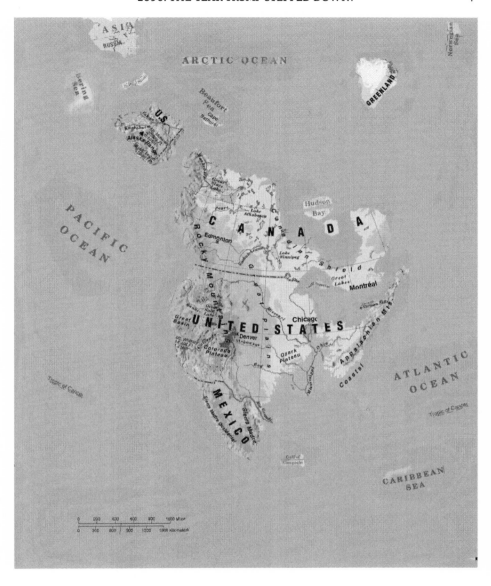

North America, 2036

Someone told me long ago
There's a calm before the storm
I know it's been comin' for some time
When it's over so they say
It'll rain a sunny day
I know, shinin' down like water
Yesterday and days before
Sun is cold and rain is hard
I know, been that way for all my time
'Til forever, on it goes
Through the circle, fast and slow,
I know it can't stop, I wonder
I want to know
Have you ever seen the rain
Comin' down on a sunny day?

-CCR

Author's note:

T his happened and will continue to happen. No, this is not some rah-rah, call-to-action speechifying; this is factual-fact.

Put simply, something different occurred on Tuesday, November 3, 2020, the day the President officially lost The United States Presidential General Election... yet still had two months left before he and his family were required to stand down. Sure, he had been impeached by that whole Ukraine thing, but that didn't mean he had to *leave* until he lost the 2020 election.

And now that he had lost the election, he had to find another way.

To stay.

Our real, factual-fact, historical tale picks up at this exact moment.

CHAPTER ONE

Washington DC, November 3, 2020

*B**ump!*— Then the "mysterious Wizard" flew away (more on that later).

For some reason, this strange disturbance caused President DXXXXD X. ~~TXXXP~~ to squash the TV's remote-control against his stomach and the pizza boxes.

He then saw that the TV was curiously tuned in at a low volume to a rerun of *60 Minutes* (which was a show he had *definitely heard* of; He had even appeared on it a few times).

He turned up the sound and watched one of the stories (ten minutes, twenty-two seconds). Then afterwards, he turned back to his own stories.

And that, dear readers, was when everything *really* started to go haywire.

SIXTEEN YEARS LATER

Brookfield, Illinois May 31, 2036

The McGillicuddys

To be at the Brookfield Zoo with her family on a bright, sunny day like this had always been Kiki's dream, even if the zoo was thigh-high in garbage-water. "Can we go see the lions?" Kiki asked.

"Of course!" replied Mac-Daddy. So the McGillicuddy family, a young, stolid, Irish-American clan of four, followed the path down, sloshing in their waist-high waders in the direction the lion-shaped arrow was pointing. Like always (of course), there was nothing to be seen in the lions' area except rocks and fake trees.

"Sometimes, the best things come to those who wait," said Mommy-Mary to red-haired Kiki with a wink.

"They'll be out," Kiki's tall, pimply, teenaged brother, Mick, assured her, "You'll see."

Time passed, and Kiki started to get jumpy, kicking at the bobbing bottles and cans (although the zoo *did* do a remarkably good job of diverting most of the floating waste away from their property).

"Don't kick the trash, honey. Germs."

"Daddy?" Kiki said abruptly, "Why is United America called 'The Big Pony'?"

"Well, because of the smaller size, pumpkin," Mac-Daddy explained. "Our country used to look like a big horse when I was your age, but then it got smaller, and now it looks more like a pony."

At this point, Mick, *very much* meaning to rock the boat, cut in: "But that was the *old* United States..."

"Cool it, Mickey..." warned Mac-Dad.

"...*Now*," Mick continued, "the *entire continent* of North America is called America-United. Or United-America (or something like that; no one's really sure). But *currently*, in real, factual-fact, everyone says United-America looks like a three-legged buffalo because American-Canada is its round back, and Mexico-of-America looks like the buffalo's gigantic penis—"

"Mick!" exclaimed Mommy-Mac furiously, the tip of her nose bright red.

"(...much the same way Italy *used* to look like a boot...)" Mick continued bravely on, "(...but now, with its swallowed-up shores, it's nicknamed *The Bootie*)."

Kiki's freckled face conveyed merely confusion. "'Booty'? Like a butt? OK, wait, if the whole American continent is called The United-Americas," said Kiki, "then what's South America called?"

"We don't like to talk about that," said Mr. McGillicuddy, happy to change the subject as he spotted something: "Oh, look, Kiki!"

Kiki glanced where her dad was pointing, and she witnessed an actual, real male lion, featuring a large, shaggy mane, ambling out majestically to recline on the rocks.

"Oh, my goodness!" exclaimed Kiki. "Look!"

"You ready?"

"Yes."

"Well, you better hurry before someone else comes."

So Kiki raised her long rifle and shot the lion in the face. Everyone cheered! A pink golf ball rolled down the chute and came to rest in a gold cup. Dad took the ball and read what was written on it, hammily proclaiming: "...aaand the little girl gets three free extra rounds at the penguins!"

"The penguins are so boring, Dad," complained Kiki. "They don't move fast."

"They do when they swim!" laughed Daddy-Mac. "Good luck hitting them then!"

"I could..." Mick confirmed quietly.

"Let's do the penguins *next time, not now!*" said Mommy-Mary, turning to her husband and whispering, "Come on, Mac, we gotta go. Weather."

"OK, everyone, time to go! We'll visit the penguins on the way out!" Mac-Daddy declared with a wink in Kiki's direction.

At that moment, however, it started to rain on that previously sunny day, *hard*, and all else was suddenly moot. The 'Cuddy family jogged/sprinted/jump-waded through the water along with other zoo-goers towards the parking area, everyone picking up speed with every passing slippery, high-water-hurtling step. It began to almost feel like a spontaneous running race, but everyone knew the race was against the gathering mud storm.

Reaching their Super Deluxe just as the heavy stuff started to come down, Daddy-Mac fired up the Ol' Hummer-With-the-Five-Foot-Struts and jockeyed for position with the others who were commencing their manic treks home in similar hi-rise, aquatic-friendly Four-Wheelers.

Lightning soundlessly streaked the bright red sky, illuminating the tornado clusters below. Then, five seconds later by Kiki's count, two *cranium-shattering thunder explosions* (causing everyone to flinch or shriek) *boomed*, signaling the actual storm was five miles away and closing. "Like giant spinning tops under a fireworks show," is how The Dear Leader once described what He now called "The Fabulous Weather Shows of The '30s." It really was a kind of awe-inspiring sight if you chose not to see the forest for the trees.

As always, "Mac-Daddy" McGillicuddy had to select his driving routes quickly through the torrential downpour, between the dozens of dirt (now mud) road-paths and byways that wound along the dangerously fragmented, earthquake-ravaged highways and roadways of old, now rendered utterly useless.

(The fractured concrete monoliths formerly known as "roads" were, in truth, little more than obnoxiously large obstacles nowadays, always in the way of seemingly *every single place anyone wanted to go*). The word "infrastructure" wasn't used much anymore. These days, you pulled yourself up by your own bootstraps and made your own infrastructure. Often though, these new, makeshift-transportation mudpaths inspired nostalgic feelings in fortyish-year-olds like Ma and Pa McGillicuddy since they mostly cut through what used to be the front and back yards of the old, dilapidated, suburban houses and schools of yesteryear.

Frustratingly, Daddy-Mac seemed to always choose the most *aggravatingly slow paths*, frequently having to detour around large houses or stuck cars. On this trip, though, only once did Mick have to get out and push, and this was chiefly because the McGillicuddys' tires were, as always, at least four feet wide, newly gnarly and knobby, highly expensive, and usually pretty damned *kick-ass*. Tires meant survival in United America today, as proved all too plainly by the poor suckers behind them who were now and forever stuck on the loamy bypaths and lo-ways, helplessly unable to budge as the superstorm loomed rapidly onward and over them.

In all likelihood, they would all be dead by morning, those inhabitants of the cars who got mudstuck. It was one-strike-and-you're-out in this present clime; everyone had agreed to that.

Because everybody had *chosen* this life. Over and over again, with increasingly large percentages, the American public *chose* this in every election since The Shocker of 2016.

Now:

Were the elections rigged?

Sure.

Was there ever active hacking into voting machines or voter rolls and other kinds of "miscounting" of ballots?

Sure.

Did gerrymandering and dark money insure the popular vote never actually "won" the election?

Yes. The Supreme Courts made sure of that. And so did the ~~TXXXP~~ Electing-College (The President re-named the Electoral College after himself in '29 by signing a bill declaring its "eternal-Forever-existence" ("Like the stamps!" He said), calling it "The ~~TXXXP~~ Electing-College Forever-Law").

Were the elections "fair"?

(An archaic term, only understood (and rapidly being forgotten) by the older generations.) The American public had simply accepted, after a while, that you had to win by a landslide these days, or you *didn't* win because the other side always cheated (pathetic shrug).

And of course, Americans asked for these faked elections because they voted time and time again to elect the very people that looked the other way. Why did America decide, ultimately, that this rigged electoral process was good enough? Some feel the answer was summed up best in 2029 by then-twenty-six-year-old congressman Jim Weymouth of Kansas when he opined:

"Humans beings don't possess the capacity to be nice to their future selves anymore."

That rung strangely true and became somewhat of a mea culpa moment for the entire nation as its piercing rightness sluggishly dawned on everyone. So... subsequently, United-Americans begrudgingly learned to live with the philosophy that they asked for: Do not make a mistake or you'll be incarcerated in the West Virginia State Pen or dead. Because unless one had enough

~~TXXXP~~ PardonBucks lying around, there would be no other chance given.

And *that's* why you had to have great, great, just *great* tires like the McGilliCuddys and a great, great four-wheel drive to boot. Or you and your family could be dead any time the need arose to leave your underground abode, for any reason at all. These daily flash-mud storms could kill.

Now: If one felt bad after losing a loved one in these newer, larger storms, the answer was ~~TXXXP~~ television. The ~~TXXXP~~ Administration would soothe its public through RAMFOX chirpees, or the government-owned RAMFOX News Channel, which was mandatory viewing at least five times a week (and the Administration wasn't kidding about that either; outside the plush, heavily televisioned capital cities, there were multitudes of bolted-down, vandalism-proof, fifty-foot-high communal TVs out in the dusty wilderness, all over the Four Sticks and beyond, guarded 24-7 by Wizards so the have-nots in the wastelands could watch too). To console grief-stricken Americans who had lost loved ones in the superstorms, the Administration would frequently remind its constituents that any grieving-type people were supposed to think on the legendary, Old West wagon train journeys of the 1800s, and then they wouldn't feel so sad if someone died: "...Because, remember, families would routinely lose four or five kids *or more* on those nation-crossing wagon-train treks! And also remember," The Chosen One ~~TXXXP~~ added sagely, "that was actually at a time when America was also considered 'Great' as well! So take heart."

So in a nutshell, "Stop Your Bitchin' (but in a good way)" were the thoughts and prayers the Administration offered everyone because they needed to stress that all of this current carnage being inflicted *wasn't* the Administration's fault, and it wasn't even that odd, *historically,* if you thought about it (which they clearly had been doing, a lot).

At last, the McGillicuddys' Super-Deluxe Hummer-Z swerved into the driveway of their basement-level house in KXCH Manor,

Rockford, which sounded fancy, but was basically a slum. Their former hometown, the city of Chicago, was gone, after all, gone like the poles, swallowed by Lake Michigan *(amongst other things)* (more on that later) and replaced with Rockford, Illinois, as the temporary, primary bastion for any open-minded Liberals left in the upper Midwest, outside the domed capital cities. The full, "official" name of the region where the McGillicuddys resided now was "Loser-Sanctuary-Dirty-Chicago" or, more commonly, LSD-Chitown (which rightfully returned to Chicagoans the fun acronym of L.S.D. since the long-submerged Lake Shore Drive was obviously gone forever). It was never fully explained why Rockford, a good eighty miles from used-to-be-Chicago, was called "Chicago" at all, but LSD-Chicago (i.e. Rockford) was one of the two places left where the BASILs (Bad, Angry, Sad, Idiot Liberals, coined by Erik T̶X̶X̶X̶P̶ in '30) were allowed to exist nowadays.

There were ten domed capital cities in The-United-America now:

North Platte-Nebraska,

St. Louis-Missouri,

Memphis-Tennessee,

Kansas City 1 (the one in Missouri. *Not to be confused with "The-Kansas-City-2-Losers" on the Kansas side*, the only *other* open-air, openly Liberal Bastion in America besides LSD-Chicago),

Cincinnati-Ohio,

Aspen-Colorado (mostly preserved for T̶X̶X̶X̶P̶ Family vacations after Denver was obliterated in the Miller-Time bombings),

Dallas-Texas,

The Rapid City Sea in South Dakota,

...and then along the West Coast:

Salt Lake City-Utah and

Phoenix-Arizona.

The McGillicuddys, for one, would have loved to be in Cincinnati or Saint Louis, the two closest domed capital cities in proximity to them, but they didn't have the ~~TXXXP~~Bucks.

Not anywhere near.

Above Myrtle Beach June 4, 2036

Ted and Bob

T ed and Bob were both smiling and feeling like they were floating in the sky. "This is the life."

"Oh, yeah," said Bob as the sun burned brightly upon them. "You got block on, don't you?"

"Oh, yeah," responded Ted, "You kidding?"

"Just checking."

(They relaxed and drank from cups with paper umbrellas.) "So no more saying anything?" Ted asked Bob.

"Nope."

"About *it*?"

"Nope."

"About Him too? Can I even say 'Him'?"

"Just probably don't."

"And this is now the law?"

"That's what I hear."

"From the Administration?"

"Well, yes. And Facebook."

"Can I even say that now? *'The Administration'*? Without gettin' a look-see from above? From 'Space Force!'?"

"Probably just don't, especially in that tone."

"And you think they can hear us now?" Ted asked incredulously.

"Please."

"Now?"

"Please."

"Really?"

"*Really?*"

"No, really?"

"No, *really?*"

"But *how* could they listen to *everyone?*"

"C'mon. You know they got little Facebookcams and mikes all over." Bob grinned at a dot on the wall behind him: "Hello!"

"Yeah, but how could they find the time? To listen to *every-one?*"

"They don't. The spiders do. And the Wizards. They do it all for them."

"Oh, yeah?" asked Ted.

"Please," said Bob again.

"I never even registered for Facebook," Ted admitted.

"Well...you have a beautiful page."

"I do? Because I swear, I've never even seen my own Facebook page. Not once."

"It's gorgeous," said Bob, smiling gently into the fearsome sun. "You have all these great, fun posts, saying things like, 'Enjoying the beautiful sunset with my love!' accompanied by pictures of us, or little ten-second videos of us, just sitting out here, y'know, 'Digging Life' or whatever."

"But I never posted any of that!" said Ted.

"Well, *they did for you.* Don't worry. Your page looks way funner and more exotic than our stupid-ass, real-life reality." Bob took a sip of his mai-tai. "And they only use the photos where no floating garbage is visible." He looked at the bright sky. "Which must be tough to find. Either that or they photo-shop it out."

Ted and Bob were legal algae farmers. Currently, Myrtle Beach was sixty-plus feet underwater (more on why and how that happened later), but there were still multitudes of energy-producing algae farms left, legal *and* otherwise. Mostly, they were tended by folks like Ted and Bob, squatting in houses perched on top of huge, eighty-foot concrete stilts, sunk deep into the ocean's bed, exactly like Ted and Bob's abode was, and hovering above the ocean like ghostly bubbles floating on miles of multi-colored algae. These structures were originally built by the government as waystations to pump water to the inland desert areas. Ted and Bob's farm, however, was *legal now* (i.e. they were paid by the government to supply energy via algae to themselves and others, plus they were paid an additional stipend to manually pump water inland to the capitals and the new, man-made Rapid City Sea).

Frankly, to be legal now was a relief to them. Yes, the Regime's Administration paid them much less than the contraband energy factions used to pay, but in their relatively old age (Ted was thirty-five and Bob was thirty-seven), it was worth the cut in pay to sleep easily. They still *looked like* typical "outlaw" energy-producers after all, both of them grossly over-tanned, featuring the kind of skin hue only seen in aging surfers or snowboard-instructors, ever in baseball caps with their sun-drenched blond locks spilling out the sides.

Theirs was one of countless adobe-igloo-like structures on pillar-stilts dotting the waters over what was now known as The Lost Cities of the Carolinas, and these queer habitations, suspended above and pixelating the waters of both coasts, were all constructed to withstand anything from hurricanes to tsunamis. Which they had, repeatedly.

The *illegal* energy farms (labeled "The Lefty Fake-Dreamers" by The Chosen One) eventually merged with the *legal* farms (christened "The Great Heroes") *through government force, yes,* but *also,* most likely, because as a general rule it's always nice to have *any* type of ruling Regime smiling down upon you, and it was especially glorious for Ted and Bob, being on the right side of the law for a change. They were actually very decent people, Bob and Ted were. Well-educated and formerly employed in the sciences, but souls do grow tired of bosses who possess zero good intentions.

"Did you check our checking account?"

"When? Today?"

"Yeah."

"No."

"I did. Guess what we got now?"

"Enough?"

A big smile. "We got enough."

The two men suddenly and very uncharacteristically leapt up and hugged in primal joy (a moment no doubt already being posted on Facebook). They finally had enough ~~TXXXP~~ Pardon-Bucks to get the hell out of there! They could go anywhere outside the capitals! Sure, they liked living above Myrtle Beach and all, but it was a little like living on a desert island; you were really always ready to check out at any time.

"Where should we go?"

"The Rapid City Gorge Sea? They've got beaches!"

"Really? *South Dakota*?"

"OK, then. The ruins of Paris, France?"

"Or we could fight with the rebels! With J and the Cantras! In Canada! Right the Wrong!"

"Yeah...or we could just live out in the Four Sticks...and battle the freaks." Bob and Ted were both silently struck by how few attractive non-capital-city options there really were.

"Could we get enough PardonBucks to get into Memphis or one of the capital cities?"

Ted laughed. Genuinely laughed. "Dream on."

"Is the rocket ready?"

"Been ready for a while."

"(Supposedly everyone's got a rocket now though.)"

"(Ours is better.)"

"Wait a minute!" Bob ejaculated suddenly. "Did you *check the checking?*"

"I just *said* I checked our checking account, remember?"

"No, not the checking account! Did you *check the checking*?"

(Bob had such a marvelously cryptic, pun-strewn way of speaking sometimes. It was refreshing. Sort of... (truthfully, it was also getting on Ted's nerves)).

— Feeling a touch irritated, Ted sat back down on his Beach-Throne, one of two raked, aerodynamic ramps on the roof that were part of the overall, adobe-igloo structure. Obviously they owned zero furniture; it would have been gone with the wind in one of the countless Cat 7 storms they had to huddle down and endure. — Ted always became upset when he thought about his dirty little secret, which he was doing right now. "No, I didn't check the waterlogged water-logs, if that's what you mean," he said.

Bob grinned way too big. "That's right! We have to *check the water-logs*, hence, did you *check the checking*?'" Bob kept staring and smiling at Ted, probably because he had imbibed a titch too many homemade algae wine coolers... And Bob also had a green, leafy, chive-thing stuck in his teeth. Quickly vibing it out, Bob asked self-consciously, "What?"

"Nothing."

"What? Do I have an issue?"

"Yes, you have an issue."

"Where?" asked Bob, hiding his teeth with tensed lips and pointing at his mouth: "Here?"

"Yeah. Just right down Broadway and to the left."

Bob wiped every single tooth with every square inch of his forearm. "Better?"

"Yeah. You got it." (He hadn't.) "And yeah, I checked the logs, and yeah, we're good for now. We should pump water for an hour or two later, but we're good."

"Cool," said Bob.

Ted tried to relax again. They would pump later. Pumping was another part of their job. Pumping was a necessity. Pumping was excellent exercise. But for now, he could relax.

Bob, on the other hand, had plainly and inebriatedly decided all on his own to commence his half of the pumping chores right now, forcefully and drunkenly cranking one of their humungous, four-foot levers as fast as humanly possible.

Great, thought Ted. *He's trying to guilt me into pumping. Well, I ain't taking the bait.* Ted reapplied 147 Sunblock to his face and upper body and tried to be a million miles away.

By 2036, there were *thousands* of water pipelines that extended far inland from the diminishing eastern coast in order to supply water to the America-United capitals of Memphis and Cincinnati, and even much further, up all the way to North Platte. So, even though scientists had been roundly maligned as *con men* throughout the country, Bob and Ted were relieved that the eggheads did get Their One Good Idea through, which was to pump the endless seawater away from the swamped and disappearing shorelines into the center of dried-out, drought-ridden America-United, pouring it straight into the deserts and newly formed, man-made inland gorges and seas. "At least THAT makes sense," The Chosen One Himself had written in one of His chirpees (the Administration bought Twitter in 2023, and then, as an act of vengeance against the former company, renamed it Chirpee). *This was the only-time* ~~TXXXP~~ *had ever publicly agreed* with "The Eggheads" (the scientific community), and it was over the issue of inland water-pumping.

After a while, though, young uber-scientists Ted and Bob grew disillusioned with the way things were. Everything was so incredibly dumbed-down nowadays, and the lack of critical, real-fact information was mind-numbing and frustrating for their scientific brains. *For example, it seemed nearly impossible to find out what happened to the Southern Hemisphere! Africa, Central America and South America were all basically gone now! And* the Middle East! *What happened? No one knew!* They were dying to know, Ted and Bob were; they *NEEDED* to know, and had desperately been trying to find out, but no one would tell them anything. Because it was illegal to speak about it.

Ted looked up at Bob's sweaty, churning muscles as he pumped the lever, forcibly shoving water through the filtered pipelines and further inland. In truth, they'd been through a lot together. Ted had been living off the grid with Bob now for almost nine years, and that included when they were chased out by Miller-Time in Margaritaville during the Florida-Canada Wars, when their unlawful algae farms and contraband solar windmills were discovered. But now, *only five years later*, they were back, on top of the Carolina Coast, legally hovering over What-Was-Myrtle Beach, "Just layin' back and diggin' the surf, and the algae, and the birds and the bees!" —Facebook, June 4, 2036, posted by Facebook for Ted.

(Which was a silly post, really. Because, of course, there were no more birds or bees left. Practically all of them had died naturally or been killed for fun or food.)

Ted closed his eyes and saw the sun peeking through, all orangey with traveling kaleidoscopic dots of light, dipping and darting around his eyelids...

He was dreading telling Bob his Secret. This Secret was that Ted didn't think he was gay anymore. If he were to announce this to Bob, *now*—that he was *straight*—there would be hell to pay and nowhere to go.

Non-Hamilton Canada June 23, 2036

J

A tightly muscled, lithe and dangerous man, dressed in military rags, body *covered with ludicrous and elaborate scars*, walked out of the shadows into a clearing, emerging into the bright sun.

One of the two captured women spoke to the man:

"Are you J?"

(The stigmatized and dangerous man ignored the question.) "Who are you?"

"I'm QT."

The scary-scarry man smiled: "I've heard of you."

"Yeah? So? You J?"

"Yeah," admitted the lauded military legend. "I'm J."

QT smirked. "We heard that you were the one to talk to 'cuz you're the toughest Cantra."

J shrugged. "OK."

"This is THC."

J nodded. "I've heard of her too."

"What have you heard about us?"

"That you were terrorists."

In the old North America, those would be fighting and/or dying words. But now, in the charred remains of what used to be called Canada, those words were beautiful. While the denizens of the posh capital cities lived out their elite, cigar-smoking-and-opera-attending existences, J and other rugged, wayfaring mercenary soldiers like him roamed the wastelands, attempting to amass armies to Right the Wrong.

J spoke, suddenly and aggressively stepping forward, looking into their eyes, "What are you gonna do to *prepare* for the battle?"

"Get Ready."

"What are you going to *say* in battle?"

"Hey Big Brother."

"What do you *want to do* in the battle?"

"I Just Want to Celebrate."

"Were you born for this battle?"

"Born to Wander."

"And what will you likely *lose,* in this battle?"

"(I Know) I'm Losin' You."

"Very good," said the ruggedly handsome mercenary in his mid-forties who called himself J, and then he almost smiled, because THC and QT knew the codes. The codes that unlocked the earth's future. Because people in the know *knew* that it was all about the rare minerals, or Rare Earth. (Rare Earth was also a famous rock band from the 1968's and '73's or whenever, so you learned Rare Earth's five Billboard top-ten hits, and you memorized them like your life depended on it. Because it did. Your code-replies were always in response to a question with the word "battle" in it. This was the way to tell if someone was a fellow Cantra (Canadian-Contra)).

The Final Battle on Earth would be decided over who controlled the rare earth and rare metal reserves *because rare-earth minerals were needed to create all of the most devastating modern weaponry.* This was clear. *And this was also the way to overthrow the ~~TXXXP~~ regime.* J and his marauders *had to* get to the stockpiled rare earths, rumored to be in Ohio, and they *had to* take them away. Or... J didn't know what.

By now though, the legendary, enigmatic J had already mysteriously disappeared into the dead dust-forest. "He's a master of the Irish exit," J's handsome sergeant-at-arms, RR, explained. "It's the art of slipping away from a gathering absolutely unnoticed. — Did you see what J did to the minerals mine yesterday?"

"Yeah, we saw," said QT (RR then tried to wordlessly slink away into the standing deadwoods, but his departure was far more noticeable, unlike J's quiet, clandestine exit).

QT caught THC looking a little bit too long. "You like him, don't you?"

"Who, that *dude, RR?*" asked THC incredulously. "Yeah, right."

"Just remember. We got no time for that."

"Duh!"

"We don't."

"I know!"

"This is some end-of-the-world shit goin' on here, bitch."

"I know, bitch! Shut your damn face! I'm focused! Shit!"

C'mon," said QT, making her way into the dark, dead, standing wood. "We gotta find out the latrine situation around here."

Later that night, sitting 'round campfires, groups of soldiers traded really-real, factual-news-facts. Since they didn't know anyone else in camp, QT and THC gravitated to J's campfire, and nobody seemed to have a problem with them being there.

(Fireside stories were important at this time since it was almost impossible to gauge the concepts of real and fake anymore because *everything* was completely subjective. In Canada, to sift out the lies, the Cantras as a rule went with their gut: What sounded and "felt" real. "Who gained from the action?" This was the question they learned should be asked to test the accuracy of any tale. If "this" really "happened," who profited from it sufficiently for the story to make sense?)

On this night, RR and another guy named Z were boasting

about seeing the tropics of Northern Italy and Switzerland only a few weeks prior.

"So wait a minute," THC cut in, speaking at the fire for the first time ever, and pretty nervous about it, "if Greece, Italy, and Spain are now the world's southernmost-countries, then where is Kenya, or Egypt, or—?"

"No one likes to talk about the Middle East or Africa, including us," replied RR.

[The following is the conversation that transpired next; no one knows who said what necessarily, and ultimately, it's not important. Only that it was said. Afterwards, a pirated recording of the conversation would be jazzed up and set to music, soon becoming one of the most famous human anthems ever created. All that is known now about this "Burst" (as the song is now known) of conversation is that it included the following speakers: J, THC, RR, QT, KIM3, Z, D-D, NTN, NME, FGYF The Creator, DRT, JOU, JOI, U-BO-The-Killer, D2, FR, F2, H99, H20, NJJV, Killer-J44, JKK and NUM4.]

"He's just one man."

"What?"

"One. That's all it comes down to."

"You know how many people supported Him?"

"Not many."

"One man."

"What?"

"Promising things."

"To whom?"

"To the powerful."

"Say what?"

"He promised things to small groups of powerful people."

"Of powerful people?"

"Of powerful people."

"Of powerful."

"That's all he did. He kept promising things to many many—"

"Many—"

"Many many small groups of powerful people."

"Powerful—"

"People—"

"To serve himself."

"To serve his own power."

"And if you get enough small groups of powerful people…"

"The Powerful Few."

"…you can rule the world."

"Then *you* have all the power."

"But that's not all it takes."

"Not at all."

"Nope."

"It requires controlling the majority of the world's greatest weapons and fighting forces."

"Powerful forces."

"He hijacked the majority of the military."

"He did hijack a majority of the military."

"He hijacked it."

"Hijacked the power."

"Cuz now He had the Rare Earths for battle."

"Rare Earths. Celebrate!"

"Get Ready, Big Brother!"

"Promises of it. To make the weapons."

"Promises of the Power. Of Rare Earth Power."

"And then anybody, any crime family, anybody—"

"Anybody—"

"…anyone could do whatever they wanted."

"Whatever He wants."

"Forever."

"Forever."

"He controls the information and controls the armies."

"Powerful."

"Forever."

"Yeah. Forever."

"Promises."

"Promises of the Power."

"Whatever He wants."

"Forever."

"So they can do *whatever they want.*"

"Forever."

"Yeah. Forever."

"But I know."

"What's that?"

"The key to all happiness."

"Say it."

"You've got to have heart."

"Don't forget."

"Never forget."

"Forever."

Then J smiled and said, "That was strangely catchy."

[As stated above, this now-legendary conversation later became a famous rap anthem, a stirring, troop-rousing standard of epically popular proportions for the Cantras and others [Spoiler alert: Yes, humans will live on in this story! (In some form (More on that later))]].

[According to various recordings] J then stated: "What it really is, is gall."

There was a lengthy pause in the conversation while the camp-fire snapped and ticked within the silence.

"What's that, J?" asked QT tentatively.

"Gall. What it really is, is gall."

"'Gall,' repeated THC, "Explain."

J spoke: "The biggest weapon the ~~TXXXP~~ Administration has always had is gall. They don't understand the concept of shame. They can go to places where no other politicians or leaders will go because everyone else possesses a basic dignity and fear of shame. Not this Administration though," J said with gritted teeth. "Listen, though: One has to have grown up seeing crime, and human spite, and family greed to really understand what I'm talking about here. Anybody grow up in that environment?"

"Yeah, I guess sort of," THC said.

"Not really..." admitted ZZ.

"Well, *I did*..." said J. "And I learned that the way to get away with anything, *anything*, is to deny and delay, like a crime syndicate does. Find a bunch of lawyers who'll look the other way, even bumbling ones will do, and then: 1) stack the court with judges, 2) control elections, and then 3) get control of the press and what defines reality. Distort what is considered 'truth.' Now, all this had already been successfully accomplished before the 2020s, so anything that happened after that, even before He got control of the military apparatus, was already a foregone conclusion. He had already won. Because He could then create and control all the disinformation that was dispersed to the masses, plus control the laws *and* military, hence control all hearts and minds. And if you've got that, you've got everything. It's the playbook on Ultimate Power that actually preceded Hitler (who was only borrowing from others). Caesar. Alexander the Great. How to rule the world. But you gotta have *gall* to do it. You gotta possess deep down in your soul an *obsession* that can endure any shame or indignity, that says: 'I don't care if the entire world knows I'm lying, and I'm untrustworthy, and have no character. Just do what I say and show Me full respect. That's all. And then you can live in My World.'"

"Yeah," mused QT, "You'd also need to be a cynical sociopath at the core. How else could you sleep at night after fucking-up things for billions of people? Just so you can get your way."

"Get money and power," translated THC.

"*Keep* money and power for Himself," corrected RR.

"Like I said, get your way," repeated QT.

"Yep," said J. "You gotta have gall and an emptiness in your soul to take over the world. That's my theory anyway. But I'm not ruthless like that. If we succeed, I can't be like Them."

"No one wants the same thing," said RR. "That's the point. This is our last chance at sanity. Us."

"Us."

"Us."

"To us!" said J, raising his glass.

"To us," shouted the remaining few dozen gathered at the officer's campfire.

"I heard a rumor about you before the Canadian Holocaust," THC said to J.

But J had already gotten up to leave, informing THC in the process, "We don't talk about the past here."

Then J was gone. Like a legend.

White Graceland, Memphis, Tennessee July 4, 2036

The Administration

A t White Graceland, the third of the ten White Houses, Erik T̶X̶X̶X̶P̶ was having an extreme hissy fit. "No!" he insisted grandly, "We refuse to let go of Mar-a-Lago; it is our home, and it shall now and forever be a fleet of Naval destroyers, floating over the Florida Gold Coast, called The Sandals-T̶X̶X̶X̶P̶ Greatest Resort in the World! (That's *with* an exclamation point, by the way.)"

"Sir," interjected the General, standing stiffly at the door.

"I'm not a sir. Am I a Sir Erik?"

"No, sir— uh, Prince."

"Shut it then, please. I shall now read the law as statuted by Myself," stated Erik.

"Yes."

"The announcement goes like this: 'Everybody in the country of America-United will *now* be a member of The Greatest Resort in the World!, Mar-A-Lago, *right now*! Because *now*, along with their tax forms, everyone will receive a 15-Percent-Off Coupon to this chic resort! Now! So if you call *now* and get on the waiting list and also have an abundance of T̶X̶X̶X̶P̶ PardonBucks to attend this glorious Luxury-Destroyer/Cluster-Float Resort, then it will truly be the greatest vacation of a lifetime. Act now! Now!' There. That's the law. Now. As written by Me. And edited by Me. Just now."

"Yes," said the General, still at the door.

"So after hearing that, you still want to get rid of it?"

"Mar-a-Lago? It's at least a hundred miles out to sea, sir. To maintain that floating resort costs trillions of dollars a year!"

"No way! I had some very precious and exillerant times at Mar-a-Lago, you goon! Buffoon! Epstein with his army of Lolitas... (You know, Bill & Hillbeast murdered him)!"

The General went on calmly, "The old Mar-a-Lago isn't there anymore, Prince. This Cluster-Float is 140 feet above it."

"Exactly! Tourists can dive down— (Alexa, write this down) '...And tourists can scuba-dive to view the ancient wreckage of a bygone era when America was also Great Again before the Liberals destroyed it. Thanks, Obama!' (Alexa, put that in the brochure.)"

"It's not feasible, Prince Erik."

"Well, We refuse your advice. And by "We," I mean Me."

The General remained poker-faced, but it wouldn't be tough to read his thoughts: He was thinking this new Royal-Titles-and-Kingly-Jargon phase the ~~TXXXPS~~ were trying wasn't working.

Just then, the Duke of ~~TXXXP~~ burst in the White Graceland Oval Office, already in a heated argument with KellyaXXX CXXXXY. "He gave Stephen MXXXXR the presidency for almost six months before He took it back!" the Duke exclaimed. 'Miller-Time!' Remember?"

Belatedly, the General announced them: "Prince Erik and Duke Don Jr. the Younger, along with Lady CXXXXY representing The Great Leader!"

"That's Erik with a "k" now, by the way. I changed it so it would be more distinguished."

"Yes sir, my Prince," said the General. "It's still pronounced the same though, right...?"

"Basically," explained Prince Erik.

"You should change it to three K's!" brainstormed Duke Don, becoming all bubbly and giggly. "That would be awesome! I'd give you a thousand bucks."

Erik scoffed: "Right. What's that buy now? A candy bar?" [The American dollar had been plummeting for a decade and was currently 1/290th of what it was when the ~~TXXXPS~~ took over in 2017.]

"I don't understand why you have to announce *Him* if He's already in the room!" Duke Don ~~TXXXP~~ Jr. told the General.

"It's for introductions," explained the General. "And it's what you told me to do. Every time."

"Not to us! We know each other! Duh!"

"Fine."

"Fine, what?"

"Fine, Duke."

"Look, it's not Me telling you to address Me like that. It's the rules," explained Duke Don. "And since you're evidentiarily playing only by the rules, General, I guess that's what you should do. Now."

The General was unsure of the meaning of this command, but Duke Don the Younger of ~~TXXXP~~ looked really, really angry now.

"Yes, Duke," said the General, crisply snapping to attention with distant, dead shark eyes and officially saluting, due to the sudden shift of gravity in the room.

"Look smart," said the Duke, growing red-faced.

"Yes, Duke," said the General again.

Duke Don Jr. the Younger peered into the General's eyes and barked at him condescendingly: "That means *Get out.*. Go! Look smart. Get out."

"Yes, Duke," said the General, exiting perhaps more briskly than he had to. Not skipping though. Not quite.

"OK, look," continued Duke Don to KellyaXXX, "Ask Erik. Erik, couldn't Dad lend *Us* the Presidency *too*?"

"He could," agreed the Prince.

"No, no," said Kelly, "that did not end well with Miller-Time."

"What do you mean?" exclaimed Don, "Ever heard of it? Ever? Miller-Time? It's like the most famous thing ever, and the greatest ode to, like, one of the greatest names in the history of the world!"

"Nice talking, jerk-butt," said Erik.

"Plus, Miller-Time made the climate change better and faster!"

"And that's a *good* thing?" asked Kelly, remembering the taste of fresh snow.

"Shyeah! None of the egghead scientists put *Miller-Time* on their timetable. 'Fifty years before the coasts start flooding,' my *ass*..."

"That's right," crowed Erik. "The eggheads used to say Miami or New Orleans wouldn't be all the way gone by now, but they never did the math with the ~~TXXXP~~-Regime in the equation, the dumb ducks..."

"Totally!" echoed Don the Younger in agreement. "We made it go faster *right away!*"

"The second We got in here! We got out of the Paris Cord of Countries—"

"The Paris Accord," Kelly~~aXXX~~ corrected the Prince, barely smirking at all.

"Yeah!" said the Prince. "That Green-Team of namby-assed countries We dissed! We got out of those laws and every other law on envinement—"

"Environment."

"Yeah!" the Duke chipped in. "We got rid of every stupid Barack-Hussein Mother-Nature-Licking law *immediately!* Now you can dump literally anything in any river! Check!"

"Stupid, faggy, healthy school lunches gone, check!"

"*Schools* gone! Check-O!"

"Don't ever believe a word the science egghead elites say about the climate... Uh-checkaroonie...!"

"And then, " added the Duke, in awe, "add to all of that the Miller-Time bombings... *That* made the coastlines disappear *waaaaay* faster...! I actually heard a statistic that We have physically changed the face of the Earth more than any human beings whoever have lived."

"I heard that too," agreed Prince Erik, lips glistening wetly. "And it's maybe My greatest honor of My life."

Kelly, who'd been imperceptibly edging towards the door, smiled stiffly and said, "Well, I guess that was the problem with the Miller-Time bombings though, wasn't it, since we lost thousands of miles of beautiful coastline before its time... Florida?"

"The Carolinas would have gone anyway!" barked the Duke, "and the Californias!"

"...plus, the Miller-bombings *did* cause a lot of death," added Kelly.

"No more than forty million!" challenged Duke Don.

"That's right! Less than forty!" shouted the Prince.

"It's a proven fact there was no more than forty million deaths!"

"Less than!" spat Erik. "Less than forty billion, for sure!"

Someone told KellyaXXX long-ago never to press the Regime on any of the following: Faux-pas, grammar, word-choice, math, typos, and policy; and Erik's forty billion gaffe certainly qualified as one or more of those, so as per always, she ignored it and smiled distantly, remembering walking in the snow on her first date with the long-gone Mr. George.

"Listen," Don went on, "*you've* been in and out of the Administration about five times, KellyaXXX, just like everyone else..."

"—Just like everyone else who's not *blood*!" shrieked the Prince.

"...Who's not blood," repeated Don, smiling and shrugging. "Most of you 'advisors' come and go..."

"We could put in Miller-Time or The Duke or me as President whenever Dad says!" insisted Erik. "We don't have to ask you!"

"And Dad's having His final surgical operation to remove the rest of His fatty anti-bodies next week, so... who's gonna rule the roost when He's knocked out on the surgery table?"

"What about Baron Barron?" KellyaXX suggested.

"What *about* Baron Barron?" shot the Duke back at her, a few flecks of foam decorating his lips.

"Supposedly, every decision's gotta be run by 'Barron' now," said the Prince, using finger-quotes and rolling his eyes, "Cuz, 'supposedly,' he 'might' be 'next' in 'line.'"

"Barron?!" shrieked the Duke. "He's like twenty!"

"He's thirty years old," KellyaXXX said calmly, "and his likability numbers are higher than anyone's."

"OK, look," said Don Jr. the Younger, "I know Baron-Barron is like a huge, heartthrob pop-star (surpassed only by Ol' Blue-Eyes Mirislav Misentolivic, but other than *him*, fine, Barron is by far the biggest star in the world... other than Dad, of course), and yes, his new album, *Utterly Barron* is topping all the Facebook charts, but please tell Baron Barron that Father wants *Us* to reign now. Erik and me. We're older."

"Rain now?" asked Erik, bewildered.

"Take the reins," explained Don. Erik only looked worse.

"I fully understand you," agreed Prince Erik anyway. "We'll ask Dad tomorrow. Which White House is He in now?"

"The Dallas Whitehorse White House."

"We'll go to The Dallas Whorehouse!"

"Whitehorse."

"Whitehorse," repeated Erik, "That's in Dallas. And may I ask You to recall to Me again, why is this place called White Graceland again?"

"Because Elvis Presley used to live here and called it Graceland, but now it's a White House, so it's White Graceland," explained the Duke.

"That's stupid. Who named it that?"

"I did."

"Oh..."

"Hey, Kelly," said the Duke (even though KellyaXXX had inched herself 5/6ths of the way out the door by now), "Russia, China, and the United-America are the Tri-Axis of Freedom, and they run everything, right? So what are *Erik and me?* Like Axis 'helpers?' More like Axis 'rulers'! We should *rule! Erik and me! And we're going to see that it happens.*"

"Exactly," agreed Erik.

"Oh good," said KellyaXXX, without revealing a trace of sarcasm or panic.

"There's framed photos of Princess Ivanka in every home and establishment!" the Duke continued. "By law! Why not *us? Just 'cuz she's hot?* Even with her new face?"

"Yeah!"

"Tell me that me and Erik couldn't tag-team this President shit!?"

"Like the Bushes did!" Erik added.

"We could talk Him into it! Right, Kelly?"

"Your father's old now and doesn't really make decisions like He used to," answered KellyaXXX CXXXXY firmly.

"For sooth!" swore Erik at her (*This royalty jargon fad is not working,* thought KellyaXXX.)

"C'mon! My father is only ninety!" proclaimed Duke Don Jr., "We could keep Him alive for decades!"

"Yeah, but it *is true,*" admitted Erik. "It *is hard now* to get Him to change His mind into other things."

"Gee, ya think?" remarked KellyaXXX, fully out the door now, bumping it closed with her posterior. "By the way, happy 4th of July!"

"Shut up," laughed Don as the door clicked shut.

"Hey, where's the General?" Erik demanded suddenly. "I wasn't done with him!"

"I dismissed him," said the Duke. "Now only the two brothers remain."

"Cool. Oh. Happy 4th of July."

"Shut *up*," said Don.

"Anyways, the General wants to take away Mar-a-Lago! So I was reading him things my staff cooked up. Here's another: 'The lineage of Grandpa Fred Drumpf the First was discovered to be of a holy, royal family from Germany and Austria.' See? So that's yet *another* reason we deserve to preserve the Resort-Over-Mar-a-Lago. —Hey! That's a good tag! 'Deserve to Preserve.' Alexa!"

"All of the above is ballistically fucking awesome, Erik. Let's talk to Dad. About that, and my thing too. The Presidency thing. That thing too. That word."

Out on the Tiles, The Four Sticks, September 11, 2036

Alice

Alice didn't know the meaning of the Word. She'd been silent for weeks now, never speaking a sound while 'Rambling' in the Four Sticks.

She'd been Out on the Tiles for years now, and in that time she had touched the walls of all ten major capitals except for Cincinnati (and all the capitals had living greens around them! This was astonishing to Alice because in the outdoor lands, everything was brown. Brown everywhere. By this time, by and large the only things left that were green had been painted that way).

All that remained in the Western Hemisphere at the moment was what Alice experienced daily: a giant, arid desert, dotted intermittently by ten state-of-the-art luxury-domed capital cities. And that was just fine with her.

Alice was considering breaking her silence. Maybe meeting someone. Hopefully, of the opposite sex. Kinda hard though, living out in the wildlands, or The Four Sticks as they were now called, i.e. the entire remainder of the country that wasn't under those ten capital cities domes. It was like the Wild West now in the suburbs and small towns left Out on the Tiles to muck it out by themselves. *We are Great Again though, that's for certain*, thought Alice.

In real-truth, The Four Sticks *was* true-truthfully a *lot* like the old Wild West nowadays, but with a little 21st-century mafia and gang warfare mixed in, along with the almost constant tornados, earthquakes and death-storms. You had to be tough to live outside the domes. You had to pull yourself up by your bootstraps every hour of every day, that was for sure.

Alice was a twenty-seven-year-old homeless, former Conservative ~~TXXXP~~ Youth who "lost her way" (basically by sleeping with and then stalking the wrong VIPs). After a while, Alice was "disappeared" into the Four Sticks and had been Out on the Tiles ever after (for some reason Alice didn't know, everything outside the capital cities was named after the songs of Led Zeppelin (who was some singer from the 1850s or something)). 'The Four Sticks' referred to the four quadrants of The American Pony's remaining land, labeled the Upper and Lower East and West Sides, i.e. 'The Sticks' of United-America. What was once known as "Flyover America" was just simply The Country of America-United now, presently little more than a 1700-mile desert of drought and death. If you lived out there you were "Rambling On" and "Out on the Tiles" (oddly, in the old days, "Out on the Tiles" originally meant you were going out all night to a fancy party or something, like going dancing "out on the fancy-tiled dance floor." Nowadays, Out on the Tiles meant you lived that party 24-7-365).

Alice sighed as she traipsed through the guck, then she sat down under a log, thinking, *This is supposedly* Ohio *and not* Indiana *anymore, so I must be close. Sort of...?*

Lightning brightened the sky to a sort of macabre yellow and purple bruise just as Alice felt a small aftershock from yesterday's shaker. Not too bad. Still, she should get back to last night's cave within half an hour. It meant backtracking, but that's just the way it was.

Alice knew the group of peeps that passed earlier was bad news for certain. "How long I'll be waiting in this gully, underneath this old log, is anybody's guess," she mused. It was a big group. Definitely carnivores, which meant cannibals nowadays, since there weren't any more animals left unless you were into cockroaches or ants. And Alice was not. The Dear Leader had proclaimed on TV in '28: *"From now on, there will be no more animals or insects of any kind in the Americans-Unite."* (~~TXXXP~~ had never quite nailed down the country's official name.) *"The only legal animals from now on,"* He went on, *"will be hunting dogs and meat-producing animals."* After this, the diminishing animal-total in America-United consisted of 90 percent belching cows (largely as a sort of constant fuck-you to The Sad Climate Liars, as well as the Gods, because, well, *Fuck you!* and *Nobody can tell us what to do with our own damn cows, goddammit!*). Another 2 percent of the total fauna remaining in the Western Hemisphere were service animals, scarcely seen outside the capital cities. And as for wild-type animals? Shot for food or fun.

The group of eaters had actually passed by a while ago, but Alice was waiting for the stragglers. They always left a few behind to gather up the young newbies and New-Ramblin'-Losers who would unfailingly come out of hiding, thinking the coast was clear. Well the "coast" was never clear nowadays. Hell, nobody even knew what a United-America "coast" was anymore! Was it Tennessee? Mississippi? Utah? What? *One good thing,* thought Alice, *Thank the Lord that, at the very least, God's Will cleared the planet of those hoity-toity Coastal Elite and all their giant sea-mansions. 'Course, now the problem is the BASILs are spread amongst us. We're still infested with Losers.* Alice resisted the urge to grunt out loud judgmentally at this inflammatory thought.

Just then a sudden —SNAP— attracted her attention, and she ducked to see who she got.

It was a hefty young woman in her early twenties. Looked like a motorcycle hippie or something. The young woman muffled her agony scream admirably.

By now though, Alice knew very, very well to wait a little bit longer, so she bided her time as she slowly drew her fun-sized, mini-AK-47 and took aim.

Sure enough, two other stragglers came out of hiding and tried to help their buddy out of the bear trap. When it was clear enough that there were no more stragglers to come, Alice fired on them, killing all three with only four silenced rounds. Not too bad, considering the way they were all squirming around.

Now only a further ten-minute wait, to be absolutely sure, then she could collect her prizes. And then another twenty minutes to drag the bear trap and three bodies back to the cave before the next sizable tremor hit and the heavy stuff came down. That all seemed plausible to Alice.

She sat back and relaxed for a mo', all the while, always-always-always keeping an eye out for other cannibals like herself. She laughed in her brain and thought, *Those damn vegetarian Losers got it wrong, alright. 'Cuz there weren't any plants left to eat anyway! What the hell were they thinking? What the hell was this country before I was born in aught-nine, some big salad bowl for them to use up? No, it was not. This is the goddam United 'Murica, goddammit.*

Alice looked at the sky. Sundown was coming. When the weather cleared in a day or two, she had to try and make it over to the communal TVs in this so-called "Ohio-area" if she was gonna keep up with her stories. It was the law, after all. Everybody had to watch the RAMFOX *at least* four times a week (not every day; they weren't fricking MONSTERS after all), or be tossed in jail for being an uninformed, 'fake person.' (FOX News had morphed into RAMFOX in '2025. After all, 'Fox'? Kind of a wimpy name. But because ~~TXXXP~~ thought the great philosopher Roger Ailes, often called the Vladimir Lenin of the Tea-Party Movement, needed more things to be named after him, He changed FOX to RAMFOX, which stood for Roger Ailes Memorial...uh, Fox.). "Had to gitcha that Fox-Fix!" Alice smiled faintly; that slogan had the power to make her heart speed up a tick or two. *Thank God He got most of the military on His side at just the right time,* she thought. *And Thank Godly God for those ~~TXXXPS~~. Otherwise, nobody in this great country would have nothing anymore.*

Alice licked her pretty chops thinking on how the tender twenty-year-old-fat-woman would taste. 'Cuz they usually just melted in your mouth.

Cincinnati October 31, 2036

Admiral Grayson Bilge

Fifty-five-year-old Grayson Bilge looked in the gold-tinted mirror. He was still a good-looking guy. The silvering at the temples came off as "distinguished," and his ab and core work was particularly paying off. "Four-Minute Abs? Who would have thought it could be done?" he marveled. Add to that his fabulous, opulent mansion in Cincinnati, the main capital of the Upper East Side of America-United, and Grayson's name being mentioned among the Top 50 Most Influential People of 2035 by the nation's top newspaper, *The United-America National Freedom Enquirer*, and he wasn't doing too badly for his mid-fifties.

Not too shabbareeno.

Grayson gazed out the window. He could barely even tell there was another, bigger window beyond this one, 1000 yards up in the sky. "That's uncanny. It really is," he said aloud to no one. "It looks exactly the same as it ever was. It's hard to believe that the real outdoors is such a tornado-and-tsunami-infested goddam mess."

Admiral Grayson Bilge knew it: They made the wrong decisions on climate. Even in the 2030s, oil was *still* king. Solar and wind power had been illegal for many years. Mostly because

1) Climate change wasn't manmade (by law), and

2) "It had always been too late to do anything, anyway." (TXXXP, 2022.) The Administration's theory was "Why have renewable-type-energy at all? Some is fine, in rare instances, but why even bother?" And yes, there were handfuls of contraband Wind, Algae, and Solar Producers (labeled WASPs, or "The Loser Hippies" by The Chosen One) selling their homemade energy on the black market, but most everything in The United of America in 2036 still ran on good old-fashioned petroleum,

as well as also something new and improved, a chemical called "immaculately clean coal." "Like a Virgin," said ~~TXXXP~~, though the Admiral did not believe the Leader had any use for virgins or females of any type anymore. Was it sort of bizarre that the Administration chose to almost completely ignore renewable energy, even when they once *publicly agreed* it probably would have helped things?

No.

Why?

Because politics. That's what everybody in today's world understood now. Better to choose a stupid path and die following it than admit you were wrong. Otherwise, what kind of a snowflake pantywaist were you, really?

(In 2020s America it was borderline impossible to find out what was known as "truth," but in 2030s America? Good luck ever finding anything resembling *real* "truth." *No way*. Least of all from the government that Admiral Bilge worked in. If the Administration ever told the truth, it was merely an amusing coincidence to be chuckled over in later years, and every person left in the country knew it. The entire government was just ~~TXXXPS~~ now. No checks. No balances. Just ~~TXXXPS~~.)

The Admiral gazed at the flash-hailstorm under yellow skies out the window-through-the-window to the outside. "That's just the way mankind is now," explained Grayson to his wife on the sofa, his wife who wasn't even here anymore (regardless of this trifling nuisance, Bilge spoke to her out loud all the time anyway because it was the one thing left that still made him feel 'connected'): "There used to be a word in the early 2000s that was used quite often: 'petty.' Remember that, Mavis? That word isn't in use anymore. The general concept of "pettiness" has disappeared because it is now just everyone's basic, default attitude. Everybody for themselves. Or die. Everyone pulls themselves up by their own bootstraps, *these* days even more so. Otherwise you're a Low-Energy Moocher and probably a Loser of some sort to boot. Or so They tell us, right?"

The Admiral smiled sadly, standing in awe at what mankind had accomplished outside of one window, and what they had destroyed outside the other one. The domes were humankind's last-ditch, most brilliant masterwork, created to combat humankind's most egregious errors.

The capital cities, looking like ten immense Epcot Centers, all had very nice, retractable roofs for opening up during the nice weather and other amazing features as well. The domes were all real-truthfully-real reported to be indestructible from all outside forces (except nuclear), and you had to be on a waiting list to live in them. Each city had a separate White House for The Dear Leader and the Regime Family to stay in as well. Exclusive, in-dome golfing clubs abounded within every capital too, especially Cincinnati, although The Chosen One Himself didn't play anymore. Couldn't really, with that pesky four-dime body weight and all, although that shouldn't be a problem anymore, ever since His last surgery to finish the removing of his fatty-anti-body problem.

The Admiral checked his watch: one more minute until he made the phone-call.

Bilge went over in his mind what he was going to say. The two next in line to be capital cities were to be Reno-Nevada and Birmingham-Alabama, but Reno-Nevada had gone under (water) a few days prior (meaning the last of the California marshland was officially gone! Yes!), so now Birmingham-Alabama was trending as the more solid choice. So. It was certainly good they had waited to see which location was better. Grayson pressed Number 1 on his speed dial, and He answered immediately.

"Hello, Admiral."

"Yes, sir," Grayson Bilge said into his cellphone. "Birmingham-Alabama is definitely the best choice. Reno is out. Clearly. Forever."

"Yes," came the voice over the phone. "They voted for me every time. Alabama did."

"Then it's right you should reward them," said the Admiral. "Are we going to use the old Atlanta-City dome for Birmingham? Atlanta is all marshland after Miller-Time. It's been fully evacuated by now."

"Yes. That would be wise. Are you attending the rallies, Admiral?"

Bilge was a touch surprised by His sudden change of subject. "Of course, sir. The religious rallies congregate every Sunday in Cincinnati with mandatory attendance."

"Do you have a pet?"

"I beg your pardon?"

"An animal. A pet."

This out-of-the-blue change in subject perplexed Admiral Bilge a little as well. There were "animals" left only in Russia and Russope currently. When American squirrels, birds, etc., became extinct because of the bug outage, a massive animal-death chain-reaction began on land. Soon enough, there were no more fish left either after the large-scale food chain-reaction in the waters occurred. Even pet goldfish were like dinosaurs now. Legend-only. So how could the Admiral have a "pet"?

Mercifully, the Dear Leader changed the topic again: "Russia has now developed the biggest army on Earth, Admiral, and clearly they want the world, Admiral. Only China is holding them back, Admiral."

"That's right, sir," said Grayson, resolving to ignore the Great One's speech oddities today. "We are definitely still in the midst of The Second Cold War." Admiral Bilge knew very well (like everyone) that because China and Russia shared a border, their relationship in the Axis of Three was much more intense. The America-Uniteds were lucky to now be a small, well-hung, buffalo-shaped island with no land borders whatsoever. And what of all of those olden countries of yore? Suffice to say, any countries like the former England, France, Korea, Japan, etc. etc., were swallowed up by Russia and The Chinasty very, very quickly.

"Well, sir," summed up the Admiral, "that's the briefing for today."

"Alright, Admiral. And remember...this briefing...?"

"I know, sir. This never happened."

"That's right. I'll say it's a rigged Witch Hunt."

"Very good, sir." The Admiral hung up and went to join his family on the triple-decker skypool. He'd promised his son, Carroll, he'd play three-dimensional water polo with him, and it was growing late in the day.

As the good Admiral passed his impressive dining room buffet, he grabbed a leg of pheasant, imported from Switzerland, and dug his teeth into what was probably once a real, living bird. Either that or an exquisite chemical equivalent. Bilge was a guy who grew up eating bugs on the front lines in the Florida -Canada-Wars though, so he wasn't all too culinarily choosy.

Once "outside" his house, Bilge walked alongside the indoor Cincinnati Lake, which was made to resemble sunset-colored ocean waves utilizing lasers and motors. The Admiral smirked and thought: *Thanks, but I've seen enough of the oceans already. You can have 'em. Oceans are still useful as barriers, but God knows we don't need the water now.*

The General realized he could use this for tomorrow's briefing to The Dear Leader: "Sir, America-United definitely has no water shortage, that's for damn sure," he'd say. "There's a lot of purified ocean water to go around too, with the pumping from the former coasts through the filtered pipelines, more than ever, so there will always be plenty, plenty of water, sir. Our waters are safe. Helicopters with Wizards are constantly roaming the seas, making sure no one's coming, and no one ever sees much other than a smattering of energy farmers and WASPS along the deep coasts. Because no one leaves from or comes to the United-Americas anymore, sir. Our Administration made sure of that."

Did Admiral Grayson Bilge feel guilty, living in a literal bubble, temperature-controlled and perfect, with the rest of the .0001 percent, while the patriots survived out there in real, real-life, mucking it out in the Four Sticks? Sure, Admiral Grayson Bilge felt guilty. But all he needed to do was constantly repeat (to himself or aloud) the one, individual sentence that was most responsible for the world getting into this entire mess in the first place:

"Hey, I've got a family to feed."

Or words to that effect. To wit:

"Hey! Why didn't you guys do something about climate change?"

—I was just doing my job, I had a family to feed, what do you want?

"Hey! Why don't you allocate money to the starving patriots out in the Four Sticks?"

—Why? Because I want to keep my job, that's why! I gotta put a roof over my family's head!

"Hey! Why didn't you guys stand up for our country when we needed you to?"

—Look, I had a choice, and I chose to support my family.

See? It was the perfect excuse for any and every action. Nobody liked hearing it, but no one could argue with it. And hell, it worked for everyone too. To wit:

"Hey! Why are all those poor shlubs in the wastelands killing each other for food? What a bunch of Losers they are!"

—Hey. Don't judge. They've got families to feed.

Works every time. All the way 'til the very end-of-days.

The Admiral rode the escalator down to the swimming pool's fourth level, where he was immediately whisked behind a curtain and briskly fitted into subnuclear-powered bathing clothes by his Secret Service detail. Stepping out of the curtained-dressing-room, Bilge saw his ten-year-old son, Carroll, smiling gap-toothed while rising on his jetpack above the wavy, choppy pool.

"OK, old man," said little Carroll, "let's see what you still got."

He really is a little tool, thought the Admiral.

Dallas Whitehorse White House, October 31, 2036

T he Dear Leader hung up from His secret daily briefing call with that distinguished and handsome man ("I'd cast him in a movie!" shouted T̶X̶X̶X̶P̶ gleefully at the Sioux City Rally), His Secretary of War, Admiral Grayson Bilge. It was decided years ago that it would be easier for The Dear Leader to receive these verbal, less-than-one-minute briefings, especially after the last surgical fatty-body extraction He'd undergone, His final one. He was starting get confused and repeat Himself. More. It was understandable, but still.

The President's Mind said to Himself: "Tomorrow We leave for Alabama to do that whole inauguration-of-a-new-White House-and-capital thing."

The Great One thought back to the time he watched part of that egghead TV-show, *60 Minutes,* in the old DC White House, back when it was overwater. That led to the war over precious metals (or rare earths), which He, Himself, coined Civil War 2. But it wasn't the north or south that won this time. It was Good. Over Evil. It was His Family that won. And They won the right to stay for as long as They wanted.

Because on January 3rd, 2021, DXXXXD X. T̶X̶X̶X̶P̶ refused to leave office.

When the elected Democratic President (the last ever), **XXX-XXXXX**, and the new First Family arrived at the DC White House with their swarm of Secret Service Agents, they found a White House guarded by almost half of T̶X̶X̶X̶P̶'s Secret Service detail (the ones who agreed to remain), along with scores of gun-toting bikers and paramilitary White Supremacists. According to Wilbur RXXS, speaking for the Administration from a podium in the Rose Garden, "DXXXXD X. T̶X̶X̶X̶P̶ is in the Oval Office still, and he is not leaving because the election was rigged." RXXS then produced a 7,250-page report prepared by Attorney General BXXL BXXR, which supposedly proved that ~~TXXXP~~ won (it didn't).

The worldwide live broadcast of what became known as "The Stand-Off" broke every TV ratings record, a fact ~~TXXXP~~ reminded everyone via tweet virtually every hour of the Eight-Day Showdown at the White House.

At hour six of the Stand-off, there were shots fired, and the resulting gunfight produced twenty-three casualties.

That was when the military was brought in, and everyone around the world assumed this fiasco would soon be over. But ~~TXXXP~~ knew something different:

Because when the US Army arrived at the Stand-off, a gaggle of US Air Force helicopters dropped in from the other direction and set up on the White House lawn, pointing guns and RPGs at their own US military brethren outside the gates. President ~~TXXXP~~ had "gotten to" them. He told specifically chosen military leaders that he now possessed most of the world's rare metals supply, and only he knew where it was, so they had to make a choice.

Are you with ~~TXXXP~~ or not?

Half of the US military secretly agreed to stay with the rare earth supplies, which was the only way to make more of the technologically superior weaponry. This faction became ~~TXXXP~~'s Army, or the Rare Earth Patriots (REP's), 87 percent of whom were from the Deep South of the then United States.

After that, the Eight-Day Showdown ensued as the crazed madman ~~TXXXP~~ claimed he would kill millions if he didn't get his way.

…And then, just like Al Gore twenty years before…the new Democratic winner of the presidential election stepped down voluntarily ("Only temporarily!" **XXXXXXXXX** stressed, "and only to avoid unnecessary bloodshed!") and ceded leadership again to the losers of the popular election.

The rest is history: ~~TXXXP~~ said he would eventually step down but kept delaying the recount. By then, however, America's

2nd Civil War was already underway. *And the ~~TXXXPS~~ won the war, thought The Dear Leader in His Supremely Stable Mind, So now everyone has to grant My every last wish, no matter what it is. Everything My Brain thinks of is made to occur in totally real-live, real-reality*, He thought proudly to Himself.

And even when what-He-commanded *didn't* happen, He simply *said* that it did, so everyone thought it was so. So it *was so*.

It was really just all so fucking easy.

CHAPTER TWO

"December"

Loser-Sanctuary-Dirty Chicago December 9, 2036

"**A**nd then who?"

"And then... Lincoln?"

"No!" Mick laughed at his sister, "Lincoln was way back at number three, Kiki! Listen: It goes Washington, Lincoln, Andrew Jackson and then Reagan! Those were *all the early Presidents!*"

"Oh!" Kiki laughed, raspberrying her lips, "that was silly."

"So who after Reagan?"

"Reagan... then the two Bushes..."

"How long were the Bushes President?" asked Mother Mary McCreedy McGillicuddy from the front seat.

"Four years together as co-Presidents."

"Is that what your book says now?" asked Mama-Mary, hiding a frown.

"Yes," said Kiki, nodding rapidly.

"OK, then, that's right," Mary affirmed. "The Bushes were co-Presidents together for one term. A father-son team. And then who?"

Kiki looked down, conditioned to be careful with what she was about to say. "Hussein...?"

"That's right," said Mommy Mary. "We used to know him as Barack Obama, but his middle name was—"

"Not his middle name," Kiki corrected her. "His whole name was Hussein. King Hussein. And the Chosen One overthrew him."

"OK, yes. That is correct then," replied Mother Mary, shifting in her seat uncomfortably while driving.

"And then King Hussein was found in a hole with a dirty beard and pornography. And then his body was dropped in the ocean. And then, later, it was discovered he was a terrorist with ISIS, and that he was from Kenya along with his wife, Kenya-Michelle. What's 'Kenya'?"

"We don't talk about that."

"Is it in South America?"

"It was in Africa."

"Well? Where are they?"

Mother Mary smiled. "They're resorts now."

"King Hussein was also the King of Jordan," continued Kiki, "a country in the former Middle East."

Mac-Daddy McGillicuddy laughed. "No, honey, I think you're getting him mixed up with another. Jordan had a King Hussein, back when... whatever... but he's *different* from *our*... former President... Hussein—"

"His full name was King Hussein the Terrorist from Kenya," Kiki corrected him. "And it's true. He was also King of Jordan right after he was in middle school in Hawaii. It's true now."

"If that's what your schoolbook says, then that's what happened," said Mary, smiling down at the green Facebook LED light on the dashboard of the car, showing everything was still A-OK.

"The Civil War 2 was unbelievably bloody," Kiki forged on, reading out loud now from her book report like a clarion of doom. "It was all about Rare Earths, and it was one of the Loser-

Liberal-Liar television stations that gave the ~~TXXXP~~ Regime the idea. It has been said that "the Left made their own bed" when the President watched an old TV show called *60 Minutes* about rare earths, and then He watched another story about the Game of Thrones regime, and even though that was obviously a fake story (because there were dragons, duh), it still somehow made President ~~TXXXP~~ feel angry and jealous that there was another world He didn't exist in, even if it was a fake one, so He turned it off."

"Maybe don't use the word 'jealous," suggested Dad-Mac.

[Author's note: What Kiki wrote in her report contains an important point. Three segments of *60 Minutes* aired that night. If the story on rare earths had been aired first, it has been theorized, He never would have seen it, and the world wouldn't have been altered in such a strict, angular fashion because again, this was the very moment when everything changed for the worst: For some reason, after a Wizard (at the time known as a "drone") mistakenly bonked against ~~TXXXP~~'s bedroom window and flew away, DXXXXD X. ~~TXXXP~~ distractedly viewed nearly one sixth of *60 Minutes*. He then immediately told his Acting Secretary of Defense to quietly seize all of the world's stockpiles of rare earths, at any cost. Subsequently, America secretly obtained five-sixths of the Earth's rare earths in exchange for its entire yearly, *nonmilitary* budget as payment. And that was how He gained leverage over the US military. Because He found out that all the most sophisticated weaponry couldn't be manufactured without these rare earths. That's what *60 Minutes* told Him, that's what ~~TXXXP~~ heard, and then for some inexplicable reason, He understood and retained it. To this day, the ~~TXXXPS~~ personally still possess the lion's share of the world's rare earth supply.]

Kiki read more from her report: "The military then split into two factions and fought each other; the Rare Earth Patriots or REPs versus the Low-Energy, Krazy Kontras or LEKKs. The Civil War 2 didn't even last that long, only ten months, with civilian deaths in the low forty millions."

"Yeah, sure," mumbled Mary. "That's why there's less than a

hundred million Americans left now..."

"Mom, shh," warned Mick.

"Why the Civil War 2 was such a one-sided slaughter has been the topic of many discussions," Kiki went on, "but all of the following facts are real-reality and not at all lies: 1) The rare earth patriots had the technology. 2) They had the numbers, and 3) They also had the luxury of using our own army bases and the current military industrial complex, while 4) the liberal LEKKs were a splintered faction of the US military, smaller, most effective only in defensively holding large Liberal areas where any significant attack upon them would result in at least 50 percent casualties to the attackers. So, the ten-month American Civil War 2 wore on until the REPs finalized such spectacular rare-metal smart-bomb semi-nuclear (hence legal) technology, that it only took the annihilation of Los Angeles, Denver, and the Flooding of the Great Lakes to end hostilities. The surrendering Liberal army spent a minimum of five years in jail, which seemed to make sense to Him in His wisdom, and life went on."

"Kiki, did you plagiarize any of that?" asked Mick. "It suddenly sounded very mature, with bigger words. 'Casualties'? 'Hence'? 'Spectacular'?"

"I changed words around!" insisted Kiki.

"I don't think it really matters," said Daddy, winking. "Just Do Your Best to Be Best."

Later on, in the slummish, dilapidated, open-sky, broken-street-markets of Rockford, Illinois, Mary, Daddy, Mick, and Kiki stood on a nearly disintegrated pavement sidewalk alongside a group of fellow Rockfordians who were clearly happy with the way things were, and chattering away about it. The McGillicuddys gamely tried not to listen to the same old tired, smug, ranting peasants, espousing their same crap:

"I mean, if you want socialism, you're gonna get shot in the dick."

"Amen."

"If you want communism, you're gonna get shot in the dick."

"Amen to that too."

"And if you want handouts, you're gonna get zapped from God, and probably Jesus too."

"And then shot in the dick."

"Probably."

"Amen and good riddance."

"Goddam moochers..."

"Taking our tax money to feed their families..."

"It's like, *Hey! Haji! I got a family to feed!* So go back to where you came from and feed your own pack!"

"Frickin' handouts to the poor..."

"And nowadays they *always* hand out all the handouts to everyone but *my* family. Seriously. It's so rigged."

Finally, Mary couldn't take it any longer. "Look where you're standing."

The two peasant men looked at her. "I beg your pardon, lady?"

"Look where you're standing! You don't see any irony in what you're saying?"

The men looked up and down the long line of people they were standing in, disappearing around the corner.

"You're in a breadline!" exclaimed Mary, almost shouting.

"This ain't no breadline. It's for free artisan-style freedom bread."

"It's a handout! For your family!"

"It's not a handout.," he said indignantly. "It's a sample."

"You're standing in line for bread!" raved Mary. "This is the very definition of a 'breadline.' and 'socialism,' and 'communism.'"

"What the goddam hell is she talking about? Is she saying she's a *socialist*? Is she saying The United Americas of Americans is *socialist*?"

"Mom, just take it easy," said Mick, shielding Kiki in her wheelchair.

The men hoisted up their guns (some directly from their bootstraps) and glared at them. "This would qualify as a clear stand-your-ground situation, lady. Maybe you should take your kids and hubby and get out of here."

Shots rang out and echoed throughout the surrounding buildings. Two people screamed and went down.

"Mass shooting in progress," said the first peasant-man, ducking down and leering in the direction of the gunshots.

"Good thing there's lots of good guys with guns here!" said the man's cohort as he raised his Magnum-hybrid-AK-47-with-the-triple-bump-stock and grinned a wild Cheshire Cat grin (that is, if Lewis Carroll's feline creation were racist, gun-toting. and living in Rockford, Illinois, in 2036). It was almost as if the man's entire wiry, dirty-dusty body disappeared into his gun, leaving only a grinning-mouth-with-weapon remaining, as it riddled-off twenty rounds. "Better start running, bitch!" said the gun-mouth. "Now! Go!"

Mary and Dad nodded vigorously, visibly quaking, and the McGillicuddy clan sprinted to their Hummer, and Mother Mary floored it out of there as fast as she could. It was unclear whether this little scuffle would be deemed an official "mass shooting" since TXXXP declared in '26 that "It can only be considered a mass shooting if the casualties are in double digits... Otherwise, if it's only single digits, then there could be good people on both sides. Who knows?" After that, mass shootings went way down (statistically at least) because it then became practically legal to shoot nine people or less at any given time, "but never more in the same hour or within ten miles of the same locale" according to the new statute, newly defining the old, stiffer "mass shooting" penalties. And, then, just like that, He fixed the problems yet another time, and the country was Great Again.

Mary glanced down at the car's dashboard and did a double take. The Facebook LED light on the dashboard showed red.

Red.

"Mom, look," said Mick from the backseat, staring at the light on the dash.

"Yeah, I know. Sh."

Red was something they'd never seen before. This meant Mother Mary-Mac was in trouble. A lot of trouble. For possible treason. She had openly spoke out against the Regime in downtown Rockford just now, and Facebook logged everything. The media giant would soon post a charmingly edited memories-collage showing Mary McGillicuddy's greatest hits of Treason Against the State. Mary had seen it before. To Madge Plainfield from Glenview, for example. And then Madge disappeared and was never heard from again.

"Is everybody OK?" asked Mac-Dad. "Everybody have ten fingers and toes?"

"All there," replied Mick, trying to smile. Mick noted Kiki was still manically shaking as she kneaded her book-report papers with her fingers to calm her nerves. Many people mistook Kiki for Mick's younger sibling, but she was actually Mick's fourteen-year-old mentally damaged twin sister. She was shot in the head in a mass shooting in '29, and then again in the spine in '32 and was presently in the process of re-learning the world's history because she had lost all of her long-term memory from head injuries.

"During reconstruction," Kiki shakily continued reading from her book report to soothe herself, "The Dear Leader ~~TXXXP~~ developed an itchy trigger finger from his taste of how simple it was to use High-Energy Semi-Nukes, as He now called them..."

"A few mixed metaphors," critiqued Mick, still quivering a bit from the shooting and rubbing Kiki's shoulder in support, "but I respect the risk..."

"So then He decided to make all of North America His," Kiki continued, "First was Mexico, when he dropped semi-nuclear bombs on Mexico City, Juarez, and Tijuana. After Mexico immediately surrendered like Losers, they became the 51st state, first renamed The American-Mexico-Losers, and then later The Mexico of TXXXP (I know at first listening, the name doesn't make a lot of sense, but when you think about it, it really does)"...

"Very good, personal turn of phrase there," said Mommy Mary-Mac, breathing deeply, still trying to regain her nerves.

"So there was no need for any crumbling wall anymore because all the Mexicans were Carouseled—"

"Caravanned."

"Caravanned down to South America, and that's when the-thing-happened-to-them-that-no-one-likes-to-talk-about."

"Did you put hyphens between each word?" asked Mick, impressed.

"OK, honey, move on," coaxed Mother-Mary, glancing down at the still-red LED (and it didn't seem like it could get any redder). She pulled into their driveway and quickly shut off the car. "Never mind. Everybody out!"

Their next-door neighbor (the nice one) was trying to shoot down an old dead tree in his front yard with a machine-gun, spraying at a consistent, even rate along a splintered line of bullet holes on the bare tree's thick trunk. "Hey there, Irish buttholes!" he called out kindly.

Mick carried groceries, occasionally dodging the neighbor's playful sprays above his head, while Kiki was wheeled into the house, still reading from the book report on her lap (to the delight of Mac-Daddy who was pushing her). "Canada was a much simpler story," continued Kiki, "TXXXP dropped dozens of hydrogen, Highest-Energy Semi-Nukes all over the former country, many even after they surrendered, rendering it a vast wasteland other than the town of Hamilton and Niagara Falls, which is one hour from the United-America border."

"And that's all that's left of Canada now! C'est la vie!" said Mother Mary, throwing up her hands, already by the bar in the den, downing her second glass of Mother's Little Helper, and then pouring herself another.

"It is assumed in fifty years, the nuclear half-life will have passed in the former country now known as LEC, or Low-Energy Canada, which featured a rare pun on His part because Low-Energy Canada has no working energy grid left now. Ha! The end."

The McGillicuddys clapped, and Father Mac gushed over his sweet, damaged, stunningly beautiful progeny. "Our Dear Leader once said, 'Home school is a treasure to be treasured,' right after he closed down all the old, public fake-schools in 2025. And it's true," Mac-Daddy added, leaning forward to speak with emphasis (with a sidling glance to the Facebookcam in the ceiling-corner): "The capital cities can have all of their fancy private schools, but I agree with the Administration: Home schooling is a treasure."

"To be treasured?" asked Mommy-Mary, smiling playfully-tipsily as she collapsed down on the sofa. "I mean, what the hell, all the old public schools are just roads now anyway! Mudpaths to nowhere!"

"Mick, take away her wine," said Dad soberly.

"Oh, gimme a *break*!" shot out Mary with a bolt of sloshed rage as her glass was taken away. Then, frowning, she slumped down, face-first into the sofa cushions. Unmoving. Whether she was passed out, asleep, or dead was unclear.

"What the hell's going on with her?" Mac-Dad asked Mick.

"She's losing it, that's what."

"Who!? Mommy?!" asked Kiki, starting to freak out a little.

"No! We're just fake-kidding!" Daddy-Mac told Kiki reassuringly.

"Seriously. We were just fake-kidding," Mick stressed to his sister, glancing up at the dot on the wall.

◆ ◆ ◆

One week after this episode, Mother Mary-McCready McGilli-cuddy, mother of two and loving spouse, was charged with dissent and treason against the ~~TXXXP~~ Regime, and she vanished. It wasn't a Russian disappearance. —And Good *God* there were a lot of Russians in United-America nowadays. No one knew how they got in or out, but in Rockford, Illinois, at least, there seemed to be as many Mikaels as Michaels. (It was a common complaint: The Chinasty citizens never left their home, and United-America didn't emigrate to Russia or China, so why did half the Russian population have to overpopulate not only their new Russope Territory (old "Europe," crappily named, but better than Eursia) but also need to overpopulate United-America!? It was like an "invasion" or an "infestation" of Russians!) — *Despite* this, though, Mary's disappearance probably wasn't a Russian job because she wasn't poisoned as far as anyone knew, nor was her body ever found.

Her disappearance matched the Administration's and Miller-Time's style much better, in other words: People go missing. Are they dead now? Probably. But who knows how they could have been killed? An illegal abortion? Mass shooting? Cannibals? Forced overdose on opioids? "After all, opioids are still on every street corner,' said every mother to every mother's son.

"Look," they'd say on the Administration's RAMFOX nightly News segment, "If a family member is gone, then they're gone. Take heart. Think of the wagon trains in the Wild West in the 1880s. Some families would lose six, seven children. Be strong."

And amen to Mother Mary.

Canadian Border December 11, 2036

By mid-December of 2036, Ted and Bob, former algae farmers extraordinaire, were at the northern border, trying to get into Canada with their hard-earned algae-gotten money.

"You know Canada's all just the Toronto area now, don't you?" asked the gold-vested border patrol agent. "And by that, I mean the town of Hamilton, about an hour north. Toronto, itself, is underwater. A runoff from Niagara Falls. But I guess in all His great Splendor or whatever, He had to make a choice. Your guy, your Chosen One or whatever. Toronto or Niagara Falls? One or the other. And He made the ~~TXXXP~~-choice. Niagara Falls. So no more Toronto. Anyway. Are you staying at one of His hotels?"

"No," admitted Ted, "we hadn't planned on our quarters as of yet."

The border agent's eyes nearly bugged out of his head. "*Seriously?*" Well, The ~~TXXXP~~ Castle-Plaza of Hamilton is exquisite. Plus, there's also the widely known, literally-real-factoid that there are no other hotels or rentals of any kind allowed in the unofficial state of Former Canada because any and all competing hotels and/or resorts are considered enemy adversaries of The United Americas, and will be dealt with as such. Understood?"

Ted and Bob nodded (still both over-tanned and wearing baseball caps, perpetually leather-skinned surf-and-ski-looking-dudes). (And no, Ted still hadn't informed Bob that he wasn't gay anymore yet.)

"We were hoping to campout," said Bob, smiling a smiley-face smile, "seeing as we have this camper-van and all…"

"No no no no," said the border patrol agent, vigorously shaking his head. "You'll be arrested for vagrancy. No. No, no. Plus, if you book a room now, instead of at the front desk, you get a 15-percent-off coupon for a future visit as an 'Elite ~~TXXXP~~ MEMBER' after you fill out these forms. That means you'd be an Elite Member at any ~~TXXXP~~ Hotel. Anywhere."

"Sorry, am I supposed to answer that or something? Yes, OK, we will do that," said Bob, taking the brochures. "We will book a room for 15 percent off on a future visit, uh, right now! Ted? You want to fill out the Elite Membership... uh... eligibility?"

Hours later, safely in Hamilton, our heroes Ted and Bob strode out of the giant, gleaming-golden doors of the ~~TXXXP~~ Castle in Hamilton, rising majestically out of the wasteland that was formerly Canada. This was how they chose to spend the rest of their money. This was their last hurrah. Canada. But how would they find the Resistance? Then they glanced across the street and couldn't believe their eyes.

Because there, in front of them, was J. The terrorist. The man they had come to seek out. In the flesh. Out in the open.

"You... You're..."

"Yes."

Stunned, Bob stammered, "We-we came to join the Fight. There's nothing left out there. We agree with you all: The only important thing to do is this. The Resistance. But how can you be out in the open like this...?"

"Don't worry," J assured them like a superhero. "Everybody's a terrorist in Canada. Me. Everyone. So if anyone starts shooting, we'll shoot back more."

"Alright, but I only have a pistol on me..." Bob admitted.

"That'll do for now," said J. "I want to talk to you. Both of you. I talk to everybody who comes in from America. It's not easy to get here."

"Just stop caring whether you die or not," said Ted, shrugging, "If that's truly how you feel, then it's easy to get through *anything*." Bob looked at him a little quizzically, and Ted just shrugged again, blushing a little now.

"I guess," said J. "Follow me."

J led them to his military camp, out in the dust-forests and dirt-hills. At the time, the Cantras were mostly inside their underground shelters, ever busy building and cleaning weapons, readying themselves for the next raid on the American border. Currently, there was some nasty black lightning blazing above a baseball-sized-hail shower, falling through the night sky with crimsons and blood-red finger-like streaks, flashing intermittently.

Ted and Bob chatted with J and RR while sheltering from the storm inside an ancient church basement. (Every dwelling Out on the Tiles, whether in former-Canada or the Four Sticks, was in a basement. The sight of unfinished concrete walls lit by a hanging lightbulb and the smell of clammy mildew was now as much an American norm as hot dogs, white picket fences, and apple pie.) "We've got something you want," said Bob, smiling.

"Oh, and what's that?" asked J, muscles rippling as he threw an axe through a bullseye at least twenty-five yards away.

"Show him the rocket," said Ted. Bob quickly scrolled through his phone. "We are in a position to offer you the greatest gift a human could receive. In exchange for information."

"Info about what?" asked J.

"Just tell us the goddamned truth," said Ted. "Please. About what happened. To everything south of the equator. Where is it all now?! *What the fuck happened*? Do you have the real info? Not rumors or lies, but the *facts*?"

"Yes," admitted J, grimly. "And what is it you are offering?"

Bob grinned like a man who knew a really good secret (because he did). "A way to get off the planet. And to live. If all hell breaks loose."

"Which it surely will," added Ted.

"Oh, no doubt about it," Bob agreed.

"Everyone's a rocket-man with a rocket-plan these days," said J, spitting on the floor.

"But ours is the best," Ted bragged, showing J a photo on his phone of their makeshift rocket.

J chewed and spat again, but not in a gross way. "Well, *I'm* not going to be leaving the Earthship when it goes down," he said, "but maybe you can get someone else off the planet for me. On your rocket. Three or so?"

"One, maximum."

"Alright," said J with squinty eyes behind sunglasses. As the three shook hands, J grabbed their palms tightly: "This here's the only thing left of any worth around here, gentlemen. Someone's word. Not money. Their word. And you barter with that."

"OK. Now tell us. Please," pleaded Bob. "What really happened? To the goddam Southern Hemisphere? Along with everyone there?"

"You want to know what happened to Africa, The Middle East, and Central and South America?" asked J, "What happened was a process called "rutting.""

"Rutting?"

"Never heard of it."

"What's that?"

J looked out a dirty basement window up into the flashing, rubescent skies. "I believe the term was originally coined by the Princess Ivanka." (J spat.) "'Rutting the earth' she called it once, and it stuck. What happened was, in the late '20s, instead of sanctions, the Axis of Freedom began applying different kinds of pressure to countries who didn't agree with the interests of Russia, China, and United-America. *Capisce*?"

"What does that mean? 'Applying different kinds of pressure'?"

J sighed and looked down as if he were dirty, and also sorry for something. "Rutting is the process of using bombing to more quickly increase the rate at which a country sinks underwater."

"Please explain?" asked Bob.

"If the Axis-Nations Joint-Military, for example, were to carpet bomb a gulley, a valley of a sort, that led from the ocean and travelled inland... and it was done relentlessly and efficiently enough... it would quickly reduce the size of that country. Or continent."

"Reduce the size?"

"The waters come in *much* faster. Ever since the poles and all the ice melted, that's what can happen. Easily. So we... made countries smaller."

"'We?'"

J nodded grimly. "I was there. A pilot. I helped. See, the first thirty years of my life were spent in avarice, hoarding riches. And then I changed. I went and trained with ninjas in Tibet at a Secret Location. Then I joined the military. I was a fighting machine. I'm told I still am." J smiled, and the smallest twinkle lit his eyes, and then it was gone as he haltingly went on: "And... uh... the other thing that happens with rutting is that, uh, the people who live there obviously have to keep moving inland, because they're trapped." J stopped speaking. He looked sort of pale and queasy.

"Yes?"

"So if a country was consistently and flagrantly going against the interests of the Axis, more 'rutting' would occur... And then more and more and more... driving all the people further and further inland as the land shrunk more and more..." J perked up the smallest bit. "Now, the good news is, this lowered the rise of the oceans by a good bunch of inches worldwide, so, in a way," J went on, a bit less tortured for the moment, "this was all helping the world, taking reportedly unwanted coastlines away from the so-called 'Scofflaw, Shithole countries' (or whatever it was ~~TXXXP~~ called them then) 'who continued to flout the wishes of the Tri-Axis.' That was the way it was reported in Canada anyway. Right before the Canadian Holocaust." J paused again. He was really having a tough time. "Sorry, but... like I said, I was there. In the Axis Air Force. Flying sorties."

"So what happened?" asked Ted.

J took a deep breath and tried to gather the will to speak out on what had become considered unspeakable, worldwide. "So, basically, we kept flooding the borders till there was only a mile or two left, total. People ran out of room, and they all over-crowded in the middle until they..."

"They what?"

"Until they ate each other."

"What?"

"All the people of color. In the world."

"Oh my God."

"All the blacks in Africa, and the Hispanic population of South and Central America..."

"Oh my *God*!"

"And all the Arabs and Muslims in The Middle East. Just, you know, the people of color of the world. They wiped out 99 percent of all of 'em. All that's left now is White. Oh, and Asian over there in The Chinasty. There's also a few Jewish patriots scattered hither and thither, but He vanished most of them too, that time he got mad at Jared Kushner over some chirpee-disagreement..."

"Jesus sweet fucking Christ."

"It sounds really bad, I know," J quietly said, tortured, almost whispering. "Makes Hitler even seem small potatoes. But some-one *did* have to give up land for The Cause. Otherwise, hundreds of millions more lives would have been lost."

"Jesus," swore Bob again, growing queasy.

"*Jesus!*" said Ted (because at this point all his brain could do was repeat things). "And that happened in, in Central America too?" asked Ted, his face a mask of disgust. "And they just...?" J nodded. "They 'rutted' the countries?" J nodded again. "...and flooded them inwards until there was just a square mile or two left?" J nodded. "...and then everyone met in the middle and...?"

"Yes."

"...ate each other? Yes?"

"Some drowned..."

"And that's why we're not seeing any people of color anymore?"

"There's a few in Russope. There're neighborhoods. Some camps."

"How could the world just..."

"Look, it's never been absolutely proven, 100 percent. Photos and videos can be doctored, and frankly, it's a certainty that everything has been. Doctored. Grossly. But I know what I saw. And did. And we're as sure as we can be that it all happened. 'The Great Rutting' is what it's called within the Administration. The Axis denies it. Obviously. But there *are* confirmed photos and eyewitness accounts and... yeah. You're never supposed to talk about it, not only because of the worldwide illegality of mentioning it and becoming an enemy of the state and tossed in the West Virginia State Pen or something (because Facebook is always listening, and the spiders and Wizards are zeroed-in on *that* shit, you better believe), but also because of just the worldwide shame of it. That we did it. And let it happen. All of us. That we let those victims, those People of Color of the World, fix things for us. Again. Like they always did. They should be celebrated as the saviors of mankind. All people of color," stressed J. "They carried human civilization on their backs for our entire run. But now that's over."

Both Ted and Bob looked at the ground with quavering eyes. Abruptly, RR tried to lighten the mood: "But *now*, the remaining land of Africa and South America has all the best resorts! They're very large for resorts too! Like two-mile-wide islands. That's good news! ...Because the native South Americans or Africans who survived there, uh, stayed to work and serve at the resort."

"*Jesus,*" said Ted, growing as sickened as Bob.

"Yeah," confirmed J darkly, "It's supposedly like going back in time, seeing one of these Southern Hemisphere ~~TXXXP~~ Resorts.

From what I hear, it's poor black-folk in white serving clothes serving rich white-folk dressed in black."

"Just like it always was," came a female voice from a back-room. "When the world was supposedly great. And so now it is again."

Behind RR, a woman appeared, ambling toward the indoor campfire by the open door. When Bob saw the woman, his mouth gaped open. "Oh...my...god..."

"Bob, Ted, this is Georgette," said J. "She's a black woman."

Ted and Bob touched Georgette's ebony-dark skin with shaky hands and cried real tears. "She's so beautiful!"

"Nice to meet you," said Georgette tenderly.

"I haven't seen a single person of color in over twelve years!" Bob sobbed. "We're so sorry. We're so goddamned sorry. For everything."

Georgette and Ted and Bob hugged, all of them crying real tears.

"Well, we found one," said J, squinting into the dying fire. "And we aim to preserve her."

The Saint-Louis White-Cardinal White House December 25, 2036

P rincess Ivanka needed a new tiara, that was for fucking-damned sure.

"Maser."

"Yes, Princess?"

"We are not pleased."

"No, madam."

"Take the goddamn catalog. If I see one more goddamn tiara I'm going to vomit blood."

"I'll take it away now."

"Who am I meeting today?"

"Brad Pitt and Shawn Mendes."

"Ugh. Brad Pitt is ancient."

"He was on the list."

"Fine. When's my speech?"

"Two PM."

"Ugh. Where?"

"Kansas City 1."

"Ugh."

"So what should we do first? Breakfast or the conjugal?"

"Maser."

"Yes, Princess?"

"Maybe I don't want either right at this very second. I just woke up."

"Yes, ma'am."

"Did that ever even occur to you? I'm still in bed, for Chrissakes!"

"Yes, my liege."

"And I am not a 'ma'am.'"

"Yes, Princess."

"Maser."

"Yes, my light?"

"You make me want to fucking mutilate myself while project-ile-puking acid. You make me want to shit death. You make me want to get on a rocket and get the entire fuck off this whole fucking planet. 'Cuz I could. I have one." (The Administration *did* have one, but the Princess would never, *ever* have gotten into one of those things and go... where?) "Now get the fuck outta here. Or I'll have you thrown in the goddamned West Virginia State Pen."

"Yes."

"I'm going to do it anyway. Put you in prison. Because I hate you. So just go. To prison. Now."

"Yes."

"Now."

"I'm going."

[The West Virginia State Pen was the only prison left in United America, and it was aptly named because *it was the entire state of West Virginia*. The Administration had walled it in around the state borders, more or less (since this particular state's border vaguely resembled a shape-shifting amoeba, they just walled in a circular area the general size of the state), creating a "Pen" of sorts for all of the nation's criminals to have at each other. It was the obvious thing to do, rather than repair thousands of earthquake-destroyed jails around the country. And it was great TV. Very *HIGH* ratings.]

"—And stop backing out of the room like you've got some stain on the back of your pants. I've changed my mind on doing that."

"Yes, Princess."

"So you can turn your back on Me from now on when you leave a room. OK? I mean, My bad, but you don't have to do *every single thing I say*, for Chrissakes. We've only been doing this royalty shit for a year, and it's a little hard to get a grasp on."

"Yes, Princess."

"Except do. *Do* do everything I say. I was wrong when I said that. Well, I wasn't *wrong*, but... *Do do* everything I say, *always*."

"Yes, Princess."

"So I guess just bring me a cappuccino with a side of egg whites and some handmade cherry pancakes (no pits). And then bring in Pitt. No. Gosling."

"He's not here."

"Get him."

"Yes, my liege."

"Now give me the fucking chamber pot and get the fuck out. I have to prepare for him. Nobody comes in this room for fifteen goddam minutes! Then bring me the cappuccino. First. And lock the door as you leave."

"Yes, Princess. Merry Christmas."

"Shut up!"

"Yes, Princess."

"And hurry the fuck up."

The Four Sticks, December 26, 2036

Alice had slept in dozens of abandoned church basements during her trek to Cincinnati. Churches were everywhere in the Four Sticks, but they were all empty now. Religion tried to survive out in the wastelands, but eventually all the faithful got eaten because everyone knew exactly where dozens of people were going to be every Sunday morning at 10 AM: in a crowded room with only one main exit, that's where. It was a cannibal's wet dream. Alice shook her head in disgust at the thought as she crept forward, her journey at last nearing a joyous end. (She wasn't *against* religion necessarily, but the pious were overly trusting and just basically sloppy if you wanted to know the truth. The churchies made themselves sitting ducks, so, well... that's what happens nowadays.)

Alice stared up in awe while reaching out to the glass.

Then... she touched the wall of Cincinnati. It took goddam *months* longer than she thought it would (weather, random shootings and cannibals, her three pet peeves).

The golden-hued buildings of Cincinnati could actually be seen through the thick, thick glass (ten feet deep at least). *Wow,* she thought, *This might be the nicest of 'em all.*

Then she ducked down. There were footsteps approaching. Either a cannibal or a rapist. Maybe both. Alice crouched under some rocks and spied out from ground level.

She was middle-aged. And approaching from thirty-few yards away. *Probably not a rapist,* Alice figured from the nervous look in the woman's eyes. *Can't remember the last time I saw a potential non-rapist before.*

[Indeed, rape was an epidemic unseen since the days of the pillaging and plundering Old West, mostly because rapes were never, ever, ever reported now. Years ago, it became clear that you could end up arrested or dead if you accused someone of rape in America-United because, after the Supreme Court passed what was commonly known as "He Said-She Lied" in 2024, there was essentially no proof of rape, really *ever*, because *"it is impossible to know both parties' states of minds before, during, or after the sexual act..."* It was perhaps best summed up thusly in one of the Supreme Court justice's written arguments: *"Who knows if she wanted it at some moment during the sexual act? What, like it never felt good, even just a little bit, even for a second?" Kavanaugh, 2026.* Add to this the banning of all abortions outside the capital cities, and America now had a skyrocketing birth rate caused by unwanted "rape-babies." *However*, the skyrocketing birth rate in America was kept in check by the soaring death rate, both now such common statistics that they even affected the ~~TXXXP~~-Jones and the ~~TXXXP~~-Fortune 500 the same way unemployment or volatility affected the stock market. The soaring death rate (usually around 50 percent each year) versus the escalating, pro-life skyrocketing birth rate, that's what investors bet on these days. When the combined SoaringDeathRate-SkyrocketingBirthrate— The SDRSBR Index—crept downwards, the market would rally, seeing it as a sign of happiness and prosperity. Even if the stats were manipulated by the ~~TXXXPS~~ or KXCHS or the Chinasty or Russia, etc., it was still seen as a positive trend. —And this manipulation was usually transparently obvious when it occurred because the (reportedly) gold dishes of opioids and gun-rack vending machines on the street corners of the capitals were suddenly and mysteriously empty for a week or two.]

Alice spotted the sun glinting off a ruddy car in the distance, presumably belonging to the strange woman. Now *that* was worth something.

"Excuse me?" the woman called. Alice wrinkled her forehead with her hands in thought. Had she been spotted? Sounded like an Olde English accent or something. And then it came again: "Hello, sir!" the mysterious woman called out again. "Could you please tell me how to get into Cincinnati?"

Alice peeked up and silently gawked at her.

"Obviously this is Cincinnati, isn't it?" she asked.

Alice pointed with her thumb, questioningly, at the ten-mile-wide and 1000-yard-high glass-bubble beside her. Then she cleared her throat for the first time in months and actually said Words: "This? Yeah."

"Great," said the odd and potentially dangerous woman. "Now, where's the door? Do you know?" Alice looked at her, genuinely lost. "The front door?" the woman persisted. "Is there a gate or an entryway or..."

"You gotta, uh, you gotta be invited," said Alice, standing up. "You can't just wander in. You got relatives in there or something? In Cincinnati?"

"No, but I have the money," came the rich woman's answer. "The twenty trillion American. To live there for a year. I've got it. Cash."

"Is that so? You got ~~TXXXP~~ PardonBucks?"

"Yes. In the car over there," said the Olde-English or Australian woman. "If you would just let me drive you, then you could show me the gate. I've driven all around this dome, and there must be some kind of secret entry somewhere."

Alice smiled. "You a Loser? You sound like you're from a Liberal Bastion. Mind if I ask? Are you from Loser-Kansas City-2? Or what's left of it after they Miller-Time it to death next week (according to Tucker Carlson)?"

"Yes, I was," answered the woman. "From there."

"So why should I help you, you fucking Loser-snowflake fuck?" barked Alice like a rabid hyena.

"Because there's something in it for you. Maybe I can get you into Cincinnati too. Come on."

The woman walked ahead...

So...

What the hell? Check it out.

Right?

Ms. Alice cautiously followed the woman, slowly-slowly, carefully, and in full reconnaissance mode with her suspicion-meter on ten. "Are you from around here?" asked the woman over her shoulder.

"No. Georgia."

"Ooh," the woman said without looking back. "You guys got it rough."

"You from the UK?" Alice asked. "What's happened to the UK?"

The back of the woman's torso divulged she was suppressing a giggle. "God knows. I've been in the United Americas for nigh on nineteen years now."

"Oh, yeah?"

"Europe's all Russia now. Russope it's called. What a crappy name... So I'm sure the UK's gone now too. I have no idea. What a peculiar question. Here we are."

Alice had been led to a shit-brown SUV parked behind some dried-out standing deadwood in a dust field.

"Now here's the deal," said the Australian woman. "You show me how to get into Cincinnati, and I'll give you two trillion American. That's worth a few ~~TXXXP~~ Bucks."

"No fucking way in God's gree—uh, earth," Alice said, realizing just then that she hadn't seen anything green in years.

"Ten trillion Russian," tried the woman.

"Nope."

"Twenty trillion Russo-Euros."

"Please."

The woman studied Alice's eyes, growing visibly aggrieved. "Fine. Five trillion yen. And I'll try to get you into Cincinnati as well. With my own money."

Alice hesitated. This was a good deal. "Yeah?"

The rich lady hesitated, then shrugged one shoulder. "Yeah-OK."

2036: THE YEAR TRUMP STEPPED DOWN!

"Cash?"

"Yeah-OK."

Alice studied her eyes. She seemed trustworthy. But in the end, the twenty-seven-year-old wilderness child Alice's decision was tribal. It was for Party. Because when it came down to it, there was no fuckin' way any God-fearing Republican was gonna be helping out the Chinese by accepting yen or giving aid to an Elitist Libby-Loser like this bitch. No way. Not if you're an RB, a Real Believer, living off the fat of the land. Like Alice. "No," was all she said.

"You... You're kidding me," the rich woman stuttered, blinking, surprised.

"Don't want it," said Alice. "'Specially from a Libtard like you. What's your name, lady?"

The strange woman puffed up her chest and answered, "Mary. Mary McCreedy-McGillicuddy, wife to Michael "Big Mac" McGillicuddy-Casey and two strappin young 'uns named Kiki and Mick McCreedy-McGillicuddy-Casey. That's ma name and that's ma crest."

"Jesus, cool down," said Alice. "It's not goddam King Lear or anything. We're just talkin'—"

"Cabbage," the strange English woman explained.

"What?" asked Alice (realizing at that exact moment it was a code word) as three people, carrying at least seven guns total, quickly emerged from behind the Hummer's giant tires.

Alice smirked and put up her hands. "And this, I presume, is the rest of the McYadda-yadda-McFamily?"

"Shut it," said Mac-Daddy, firing a warning shot from a silencer on his hip, narrowly missing Alice's ear.

"OK. Fine. I know where the underground gate probably is," asserted Alice. "I'll take your deal. For the yen."

Mother Mary stepped up to Alice, speaking words of wisdom: "No, you'll get naught. You're a liar. You're not for the greater good. You're for yourself. You had your chance. For some money. To feed yer family. If'n ya got one. But now that fat chance is gone. So you get nothing. Now let it be, missy, because you're coming with us."

Mick and Mac-Daddy accompanied Alice at multi-gunpoint and forced her into the back seat of the Hummer. (Mother-Mary had recently found herself in times of trouble. So a week ago, rather than be taken away, never to be heard from again, she stole the family car and drove out into the wilderness towards Cincinnati by way of Indiana. The note she left behind said she loved her family more than herself, and that's why she had to go Out on the Tiles and try to get medical-mental help somewhere. Because she cared too much, and she couldn't pull herself up by her own bootstraps in the normal way anymore. So she was pulling herself up with tough love and choosing to save her family. ...Or so she thought. Because her clan was having none of it. The McGillicuddys liquidated all the family money and sought her out. And found her. And here they were, all together now. Outside Cincinnati).

Mother Mary smiled and cocked her shotgun. "Now let's go to Cincinnati."

"Fuckin' Liberals..." mumbled Alice.

Cincinnati Proper December 27, 2036

A dmiral Grayson Bilge's mind raced as he wound through the cobblestoned backstreets of Cincinnati on foot.

He had never received an order like this before.

Destroy one of the Kansas Cities. (*2. The so-called 'Loser-One.'*)

With a full nuke.

Was this it? Had "*that time*" come when The Chosen One finally went too far?

Was this *that time*?

Was this the end, either of the ~~TXXXP~~ Regime or of the world? Do we *really* have to decide *everything*, like, *Right Now*?

It was clear Admiral Grayson Bilge needed to talk to Dr. Theodore from NASA. Last the Admiral had heard, the rocket scientist and cosmologist was out of a job. But it was time. He needed their spaceship. Yes, he knew "everyone was a rocket-man with a rocket-plan" nowadays, but Bilge's NASA-sanctioned (partially and unofficially) spaceship had the best chance of any.

"The rocket" was a secret project of the Admiral's over the last decade. The idea was to build a transportation device that could travel twenty million light-years in the span of around twenty earth-years.

And the ship was reportedly ready. Admiral Grayson Bilge planned on being one of the passengers.

Now in the seedier section of Cincinnati, the sketchiest of its slums, Bilge stepped past a stunning hanging-garden arrangement spilling off one of the city's many handsome, golden gaslights, then, after passing a few art galleries, he ducked into the private alcove of a beautiful, wooded grotto in what was commonly known as The Ghetto of Cincinnati, or its more official name, "The Arts District." Stooping, hunched, Bilge plugged his phone into a random park bench. Only then did Grayson Bilge feel safe enough to dial his burner phone and begin Plans B thru Z. "Dr. Theodore?" he asked.

"Admiral!?" The doctor sounded surprised.

"It's time."

"What? Why?"

"It's *time*."

"When?"

"Within three days. Maybe less."

"*WHAT?!*"

"Doctor."

"What the hell!?"

"Doctor, time to calm down and move. Right now. Where is it?"

The doctor let out a shaky sigh. "It's uh, in an old hangar near Aspen."

"Can you be here with it before noon, Tuesday?"

"If you help me."

"Obviously. Where is it?"

"OK. Uh... Get your biggest transporter to Grand Junction. It's a building that spans four blocks off Colorado Road; you can't miss it. Bring the ship along with every single thing in the building. Every computer, every document. Shouldn't be hard. There isn't too much."

"Will do. See you soon."

Grayson Bilge hung up and stared nostalgically at the passing peacocks and flamingoes wandering amongst the giggling white ghetto children in their gold-trimmed uniforms, playing on the inner city's new playground. Rising to leave the skid row grotto, he smiled absently at a doggy-shaped, robot park-cleaner, and he fed it his burner phone, privately celebrating. Because Admiral Grayson Bilge was going beyond Mars.

Mars was a Loser's Mission, thought Bilge as he hurried home.

It turned out exactly the way all the naysayers said it was going to: a big damn bust. Mars was unlivable. And freezing. Oh, and you couldn't breathe. Why was it ever considered a Plan-B Planet? The last Mars Mission astronauts spent 94 percent of every day in their oxygenated, conditioned living quarters. If you're going to exist that way, why not just colonize the moon? It's also unlivable, but at least it's warmer and next door.

Luckily, Admiral Bilge and Doctor Theodore had different plans entirely, plans that had not only been denied by the Administration, but had been mocked and laughed out of the room. All it took was a single moment of eye contact between Secretary of War Bilge and a young scientist named Dr. Cliff Theodore while the rest of the room laughed it up with Leader ~~TXXXP~~, and in an instant a brotherhood was born between the two men, based on their shared belief that *this was one of the three or four most important decisions in the annals of humankind: The decision to create a last chance to sustain the human species for longer than twenty years.* The odds of the plan working? Better than 50-50.

The plan? To colonize the only plausibly livable, relatively nearby planet yet found: Gliese 667 Cc, an exoplanet with a 6,000 mile radius, orbiting within the "habitable zone" of the red dwarf star Gliese 667 C (a member of the Gliese 667 triple-star system), approximately 22.18 light-years away from Earth in the constellation of Scorpius. There was a strip of land discovered towards the center of Gliese 667 that the Admiral had been watching with great interest over the last decade, and if they could get a half-dozen or more humans there alive, there would be a better than 80 percent chance of the human race surviving a WEE (World-Ending Event) on Earth. Dr. Theodore claimed this trip could be accomplished in 22.4 years of Earth time. Plus, he explained once to the Admiral that the 'time dilation', explained in Einstein's theory of relativity, would make the trip shorter from the travelers' perspectives, *so to them it will only seem to take 6.2 years!*

Not too shabbareeno!

But when Dr. Theodore discovered how to build the matter-antimatter drive (where hydrogen and anti-hydrogen mix in a combustion chamber, converting matter to energy at 100 percent efficiency), *then* it all really became *truly plausible*.

They built the rocket in the style of the old John Cash song from the 1920s or '40s, "One Piece At A Time," by basically stealing, weekly, from NASA, most of the expensive, tough-to-make rocket parts for as long as Dr. Theodore worked there. After he left, they contracted-out the remaining pieces of the rocket, or else made them by hand. Since they needed more than 500 times as much mass in fuel as the actual rocket itself, the trip included stops at Mars and 512 other destinations along the way. Over a decade ago, Bilge and Theodore sent out energy-efficient lower-speed Wizards into space that carried and dispensed high-density energy pods (each containing 82 percent of the sun's power) for their rocket to collect along the projected path to Gliese.

And now, *today*, The Chosen Great One had told Bilge the incredible news that now required the Admiral to skulk around in the seamy underbelly of Cincinnati to make his panicked call. The news ~~TXXXP~~ told him (during their non-existent daily briefing) was that one of these catastrophic, World-Ending Events would initiate in just over forty-eight hours. The bombs would fly. Everywhere. *To* Russia, *from* China. *Everywhere*.

If America-United got the jump on the competition, though, *that* could be the difference between winning and losing.

But what would be left?

For Earth's inhabitants, there would be next to nothing. Those who survived the nuclear holocaust would live like the cavemen.

Grayson Bilge's plan, on the other hand (selfish and self-serving, yes, but he did have a family to protect), was for the Admiral and his son to be flying, along with Dr. Theodore and a few others, in their spaceship, far away from this planet that would essentially be a dead, radiation-tainted orb for many, many years.

Say a million folks survived the WEE... And then in five years, between weather, radiation-poisoning, shootings and cannibalism, say there were still a thousand people left on Earth, all scattered amongst the world's few most powerful groups.

Those humans could also attempt to start anew. So there was always *that*... which could extend the existence of the human race as well...

There was *also* a particular underground bunker under the old, underwater Washington DC White House property that would allow over two dozen people to shelter from possible incursions or disasters on Earth, including nuclear. But the inhabitants would have to live down there for years. Miles inside the Earth's crust. Without killing each other. And even the Admiral wasn't of a lofty enough status to get a ticket to the underground White House bunker. Not even close. He even knew that *Miller-Time* hadn't gotten a seat. Probably because there'd be a good chance that in a few years, Stephen MXXXXR would emerge from the bunker, alone, like Rambo, smeared with blood and slithering and worming upwards to the crust's surface to be crowned the Saviour of the World and King of Mankind. Nope. Couldn't be done. Everyone saw it in the White House meetings; Miller-Time could *not* be included in the Elite bunker. Plus, he'd drive everybody slowly crazy anyway.

The Admiral finally arrived, jogging and sweating at his mansion (in the nicer section of town). It was safe here; Facebook-surveilled with alarms and roving Wizards, the whole lot. The Facecam scanned the Admiral's face, and the front door opened into a 2000-square-foot living room with high, gold-inlayed, carved ceilings. As always, the house reminded him of his wife who was discovered to be a Liberal and was "put out to pasture" by Miller-Time in '31.

He smiled at her, on the couch again. He didn't like to think about it.

So he fixed himself a cosmo. Bilge, Theodore, and a handful of others would be the ones to pull the human race up by its bootstraps when the going got rough, allow the species to survive.

By going to another planet.

Because humans were factually-and-truthfully too immature to take care of the old one. They had killed it.

And that would be fine... Someone had to be the one to stand up on their own two feet and live on.

"...And that made us Great Americans," the Admiral said, toasting himself.

Rapid City Gorge White House, December 29, 2036

Stephen MXXXXR chortled as he charged down the hall. "Well, it's been sunny, so if that's what the darkies wanted, that's what they got. And by darkies, I mean no offense to you, Cardinal Mbota. The word 'darkies' refers to the population of any impoverished country because a) They live outside of the capital cities 'in the dark woods and such,' hence, 'darkies,' plus b), They've <u>chosen</u> to live 'in the dark,' unschooled and intellectually deficient, ergo again, the term darkie. And lastly, c), Because these darkies, as it were, live outside the capital domes, their skin has become browner from exposure to the real sun, ergo, my usage and seeming prolixity of the term 'darkie.' Again, no offense intended."

The pitch-black-skinned African Cardinal Mboto, walking behind Miller-Time and trying to keep up, nodded and spoke to his translator in his native Kenyan. The translator turned and smiled humbly at Miller-Time. "The Cardinal would like to thank you for this clarification but wonders how it is relevant to his question to you, 'How's the weather?'"

Stephen MXXXXR shrugged. "Well, the weather's been hot, so I thought that's what you guys liked. The sun. Never mind, off-color joke. Not "off of" color, but off-color. Just... Lost in translation!" He guffawed loudly once as the two Kenyans mumbled to each other, then the translator translated again:

"The Cardinal thanks you again for this clarification and offers that you are the whitest-shaded man he has ever seen in his life! Congratulations!"

The Cardinal smiled kindly and laughed politely as Miller-Time reddened and guffawed again while opening a door, ushering them into the White House's Iowa White-Hawkeye Sitting Room (a naming error to be addressed later, since they mistakenly thought Rapid City was in Iowa, not South Dakota; presumably, they mistook it for Cedar Rapids, which was unfortunately overrun by cannibals now).

"Well, I thank you," laughed Miller-Time. "I'm the whitest guy he's ever seen, huh? Thank you. I thank you for saying that, Cardinal. I appreciate that. Thank you for those kind words. I'll take it. I'll take it." After a while, everyone's polite laughter subsided, and MXXXXR returned to what he did best: diplomacy. In this case, it was regarding reparations with the now-absent continents of Africa and South America. "So what we're talking about here," began MXXXXR as the Kenyan translator quietly mumbled in the Cardinal's ear, "what we're talking about is a grave injustice that Mother Nature laid down on you guys. And we want to help. So: We'd like all your remaining rare earths in exchange for a place at the table. After the End. Of Civilization as we know it. I know, big stakes." Miller-Time grinned sheepishly and tried out a Kenyan accent: "What to do, what to do?"

The Cardinal knew exactly what this all meant. Extinction. This was not an idle threat. "Yessir," the Cardinal said humbly in English, bowing his head.

"You betcha," said Miller-Time, already headin' out the door. "Now I gotta go, but you stay here, and I'll get one of my indentured-servant assistants to dot the i's and all that. Just kidding, of course. No offense. Ciao."

Miller-Time rapidly skulked back down the hallway, scowling as he simultaneously roused himself: *Diplomacy-time is over. Now it's Miller-Truth-Time,* he thought aggressively while plowing furiously past the random denizens of the hallway who either stared or averted their eyes, all of them sharing a common fear of Miller-Time. *Good,* he thought. *Fear is good.*

It was staggering, the sheer carnage and destruction left behind by MXXXXR's Special Army, "Miller-Time" (at first a trademark infringement, but it was a surprisingly easy affair to have the Administration simply buy the entire Miller Brewing company. Problem solved). The Miller-Time Bombings were compared favorably with General Sherman's March to the Sea at the end of Civil War 1. There was nothing left of the Loser-Liberal Coasts after Miller-Time, or any of its previous Liberal Lairs and Bastions. In fact, most of the America-United country was in ruins now, thanks to Miller-Time. Combined with Fun-Fracking, it was responsible for 87 percent of America-United being deemed "unlivable" by… well, everyone ("Fun-Fracking," i.e. "fracking" but re-branded by ~~TXXXP~~ in '24, was certified 'Completely Safe' by the Acting EPA Chief. However, Fun-Fracking For Oil could still *never* be practiced within 200 miles of any capital city, for reasons never explained. The entire rest of The American Pony, though, was officially stamped "SAFE TO FUN-FRACK" by the Administration. After that, there was never any point in using *any* tap water outside the capitals. At all. Ever. Once a person in Georgia turned on their kitchen faucet and a bunch of black sludge spilled out with a condom in it. Although, then again, maybe that was decades ago).

Still. It was a risky political decision for MXXXXR, his carpet-bombings of the American coasts, but it ultimately paid off, seeing as everyone knew that anything not under a dome was not going to survive for long anyway. The air was practically unbreathable on the outside by that time. Water untouchable. *Thanks, Obama!* thought Miller-Time with a smirk, and then he laughed out loud and thought, *That's funny because it's true.*

Stephen MXXXXR charged down a different hallway as his mind continued to wander like a rogue, runaway train: *And where is Hussein Obama now?* he thought as he neared the Oval Office, smiling twerpily. *Oh yeah, his head is on a pike outside the Dallas Whitehorse White House, along with Colbert, Maher, Stewart (both John and Kristen), Chrissy Teigen and Rachel Maddow* (These were all old-timey dissenters of the President, along with dozens of other skewered fellow Libtards, including ~~TXXXP~~'s three ungrateful ex-wives). *Best of all*, thought MXXXXR with a tiny tingle in his stomach, *because Miller-Time's March on the Left turned out to be SO successful (plus, the actual March was in March; how organized did that look?), I, Stephen MXXXXR, was allowed to be Interim President for six months during The Great Leader* ~~TXXXP~~*'s second, big surgical procedure when He had hundreds of pounds of fatty-body extraction. It was awesome to be President!*

He smiled, knowing he was always next in line for the head job. If he was "needed." And right now, Miller-Time was going to see The Man.

"He's expecting you, sir," said a Secret Service agent named Bruno, opening the Oval Office door.

Miller-Time stormed in, mumbling, "I know, I know…"

"Stephen 'Miller-Time' MXXXXR!" crowed The Leader of the Free World, The President and Dear Leader, DXXXXD X. ~~TXXXP~~. "Glad you're here! Listen. I need to speak with Wilbur RXXS toot-sweet."

Miller-Time blanched. "That's why you called me here? You want me to carry you over to Wilbur's room?"

"Yeah, but let's talk first. Walk me around the office a little."

MXXXXR smiled stiffly and proceeded to wheel the President 'round and 'round the Oval Office while the President spoke to him: "Stephen, following My last operation, after they removed the entire remains of My fatty-body and left Me as this head in a jar, I was watching you."

"Oh?"

"And I know you were watching Me too. Because you thought you were going to get My job, didn't you?"

"But, sir. Wasn't Miller-Time successful as President?"

"Yes, you were," said Donald X. ~~TXXXP~~'s head in a jar, "but I really don't think this whole thing has slowed Me down one bit. Being only a head now and all… OK, let's get to the Cabinet room."

"Sir," said Miller, rolling his eyes while wheeling him out the door, "if I can be blunt, you secretly but *legally died* three years ago. Yes, this is your actual, old head floating in formaldehyde and hooked up to a computer, but the technology for the cryogenic reanimating of heads *could be better*, don't you think, sir? It's still practically in its infancy! Everything I read in the trades says that these are not even your own new thoughts or ideas you are currently espousing! It's the computer memory they attached, which is simply repeating every sentence and thought you've ever had before! So, in essence, sir, for years since your secret death, we have just been repeating every decision you ever made, over and over. I mean... is that change, sir?"

"So? Who wants change?" asked The Dear Leader's sound-box rhetorically, "Is everything so bad? No! It's Grrrrr-eat!"

"Yes, but... When are we going to try some new blood (...Again...?)? Just for a change. You *are* slowing down now, sir. Since you died. You must admit it. You can't really make decisions like you used to."

"How ya doin', Ted?" said ~~TXXXP~~'s head as his jar was wheeled into the cabinet room.

"Hello, Mr. President!" said the severed head of old 1940s baseball legend, Ted Williams, sitting on a shelf.

"Hey, Walter," chimed The Chosen One's head.

"Hello, sir," said the cryogenically frozen head of Walt DisnXX (Ted Williams and Walt DisnXX were among the first to cryogenically freeze their respective noggins in the olden days, so when the reanimating processes improved, contracts usually being first-in, first-out, these two legends from the 1949s and 1972s were reanimated first. Sort of like boarding for Premier Travelers. So ~~TXXXP~~ let them hang out with Him. They were good joes, after all. From olden times when everything was at least As Great, just like it was now. Plus, they were all in jars of minus-160 degrees Celsius liquid nitrogen (definitely *not* "formaldehyde"), so they had something in common to talk about).

~~TXXXP~~'s head said, "I need to see the rest of my cabinet. Now."

"Sir, they're scattered all over the Big Pony as we speak," whined Miller-Time. "They're in *all* the different White Houses
—"

"No, I need to see the rest of my *cabinet*. The place where you store me, on the shelf with the others. I've been told the cabinet was restored, but I can only see the right half of it from inside my jar over here."

"Oh yeah, baby," said Teddy Baseball. "They did a good job with it. Lookit this, *baby!*"

Stephen MXXXXR placed the President's head next to Wilbur RXXS's on the third-highest shelf of the newly restored, priceless, antique Reboulet cabinet supposedly used as a bookshelf by none other than Thomas Jefferson.

"Hello, sir," said Wilbur RXXS.

"Good morning," the Dear Leader's head spoke through the computer's dual-speaker, "Yeah, it looks nice. The cabinet. Real classy. Now. The reason I've brought you all here today is this. We gotta nuke 'em. The last of the naysayers. The last of the non-believers. The Losers. We've got them all crowded into two places now: Loser-Kansas-City-2 and LSD-Chitown in Illinois. We should pull off both Band-Aids. With two real-nukes. No more of all this semi-nuke bullshit."

Miller-Time and Wilbur RXXS said absolutely nothing. Nuking our own country. This was a first.

"Oh. And we're also fully nuking China and Russia. Cuz they're fully nuking us. It's already in motion, and I already told Secretary of War, Bilge. It's done. Too many red lines have been crossed by everyone. That is all."

Miller-Time slowly wandered out of the room in a daze. He turned to the Secret Service Agent in the hall. "What's your name? Bruno?"

"Yes, sir."

"Bruno, come with me," said Miller-Time. "I've got a proposition for you."

CHAPTER THREE

"The Day The TXXXPS Stepped Down"

Cincinnati, Tuesday, December 31, 2036

They were finally inside. Cincinnati. And the McGillicuddys were somehow still all together, crowded in their 'Cuddy Super Deluxe, which the Cincinnati-Dome border-patrol was now telling them to turn off.

"Turn off the car?" asked Mother Mary through the car window.

"Obviously, ma'am," called the border-patrol officer in the orange jumpsuit and gold helmet. "You're in a dome. Please turn off your car and wait, ma'am. We'll get to you soon."

Mary turned off the ignition of the car into a way-too-quiet, tinny, key-jingling silence. She broke it with a heavy sigh. "Well, shite, I'm leaving the radio on," she said, switching the knob.

"Mom!" scolded Kiki.

"Sorry for cussing, honey; Mommy Mac's just been a little stressed out."

"...But this is all good news because it shows us that we're being rewarded for our efforts, for being Good and not Bad. And in this way, more of us are then allowed to live."

"*It's true, in real, real-life reality,*" said the second voice on the radio, "*It's God-like, this forgiveness of our sins by The Dear Leader. And remember, these market rallies are usually always considered the salad days of a civilization, the days when everyone most roundly agrees that The ~~TXXXPS~~ and the Axis of Freedom were and are the greatest leaders in the history of the world.*"

"I gotta admit," said Mac-Daddy, "I don't know why we're doing this."

"Mom, you're in trouble. They're going to arrest you," Mick said worriedly.

"We've got our family's entire liquidated fortune, twenty-two trillion dollars," stated Mary calmly. "My daddy Mack was rich and left me a lot when he passed. That's equal to twenty-two PardonBucks. Hence, I'm pardoned; plus, we get to live for a year in this beautiful city! It's worth a shot. We have no choice! We've got to try! I mean, this is exciting! Right?"

"*We are living in the salad days, people. Greatness. Again. And that's why we play only His favorite music on WAS, number 99 on your dial... All the time! Huey Lewis and the News, Phil Collins, 3 Doors Down, the country stylings of the Guzzlers, and KISS to name only a few. — It's 27 after the hour, on WAS Freedom Radio, I'm Alex Jones the Third...*"

"*And I'm Fabulous from the TV show* Star Warriors, *filling in for Scarlet, The Conservative Vampiress of Freedom.*"

"Just leave the radio off," grumbled Alice from the back of the SUV Hummer.

"You just shut it, missy," ordered Mary. "We could have left you on the outside with no remuneration at all. Now if you want your payment, you'll sit back there and keep your pie-hole closed. Sorry, Kiki."

"It's okay," said Kiki, glaring cock-eyed at Alice.

"I didn't think they'd ever let me in here," assessed Alice, peering around at the long line of cars they were in. "I don't know if I like this."

"Well, you can just see your way out of Cincinnati anytime you please," answered Mary Mac.

Alice grunted. "Well, this is taking for-goddam-ever. I'm takin' a nap."

"Good idea!"

"...and for all you people who bring up the old, Mythical Hitler Fables as a cautionary tale..." a third voice on the radio, fourteen-year-old Fredo Giuliani chimed in, "always remember that Our Administration is very different from dictatorships of old, whether they were real or imagined like the Nazis... Think about it: The ~~TXXXP~~ Regime was never afraid of books, like other autocracies were... Our Chosen Regime just shrugs their collective shoulders at the uselessness and impotence of the written word, and that equals more freedom for you and me! To peruse what we want!"

"...And rightly so..."

"...Because when you have the modern weaponry that we possess, the masses and masses of guns owned by each self-policing, stand-your-ground citizen, you know that any SBIs, any Sad, Bad Ideas, will be rutted out... and those persons will be stamped out immediately, whether by gun or opioid-murder."

"OK, easy now!"

"Sorry, 'ALLEGED' opioid murders—" (Laughs from the symposium). "Look around, though! All of the digital libraries remain open, and very few books were banned or burned. This is His gift to us."

"Yeah, right," mumbled Mary. "The 'Regime' considers themselves Intellectuals, but people can be shot if they use too many four-or-five-syllable words like 'veterinarian' or 'oscilloscope.'"

"Speak English," mumbled Alice, reclining in the back.

"Mom, shut up," commanded Mick, reaching from the backseat to flip off the radio while pointing at The Facebook Light in the car's dash (which had remained distinctly red). The family had already been worrying nonstop about Mother Mary Mac being taken away. Mick couldn't believe that his mother was digging her own grave even further.

"God, this is taking forever," mumbled Mac-Daddy. "Oh, I've got an idea! Kiki, read a little from your book report!"

"*C'mon!*"/"NO!"/"<u>What</u>!?" said everyone else in the car.

"This line is intolerable," said Mary. "I'm going to ask if we can go to the bathroom." And before the family could say a thing, Mommy Mac was out the door and talking to border-patrol, then gesturing them all out of the car.

So the three other McGillicuddys were allowed to accompany Mother Mary to the beautiful, golden, common toilet building while the border patrol agents continued their vetting of the other automobiles in line.

After their 'business' was finished, the four McGillicuddys found themselves standing and staring in awe at the rich capital city's shining-gold opulence: the ornate pristine buildings (because of frequent earthquakes, none above ten floors, and all mounted on giant, twenty-foot wheels) and hundreds of old white men in electric golf-carts zooming down the brick and cobblestone roundabouts and artisan-mowed cul-de-sacs.

"Mother of God," swore Mary, "can you believe how nice it is in here while we gotta scrape by outside in the squalor?!"

Killing another few minutes, Mother-Mary, Daddy-Mac, Mick and Kiki walked down the gleaming, gold streets of Cincinnati. Mick looked 'round and whispered to M-Daddy, "Should we run?"

Mac-Dad chuckled nervously and whispered back, "No, darling, they would catch us in three minutes. See all the cameras? We're like fish out of water here. Look at us!" Indeed, the McGillicuddys were presently all very soiled from the outside world and plainly dressed, contrasting sharply with the mod, sleek fashions of 2036 Cincinnati, especially the passing pedestrians' shirts and eyes, which declared plainly to one and all that the new, trending fashion involved 1) ultra-shiny gold lamé, and 2) black, raccoon-like makeup smeared around the eyes and cheeks of men and women alike, making them resemble death masks.

At an intersection, Mother-Mary spied a gold dish filled with pills, attached to the traffic signal's pole, right below the button to cross the street.

"Jesus, just like they said…" muttered Mary. "There are opioids on every major street corner in the cities. In gold dishes."

Kiki reached for one of the 'candies' in the dish just as Mary noticed a red box containing a fully stocked gun rack behind glass reading "Break in Case of Emergency." Below, on the sidewalk, was a small, fanciful gold box full of used firearms with a sign, "Take One, Leave One."

Suddenly seeing Kiki reaching for the pills, panicked, Mary forcefully grabbed Kiki's hand away from the dish while raving to Mick and Mac: "Opioids and guns. Everywhere! For free. Oh boy! Clearly, they found what weeded out the riffraff toot-sweet! Oh boy, they did!"

"What the Hecuba are you going on about, you batty Scottish git?" mocked a tuxedoed passerby within a drunken group that clearly seemed to be heading to a gold-themed wedding.

"Nothing," asserted Daddy McGillicuddy. "Just move on, thank you."

"If you make one mistake, it's over!!" Mary rambled on, wandering over to a group of restaurant-going Mods, dining under an Ohio/Russo-themed sidewalk awning. "—And then you're gone nowadays…! *Gone!* One mistake!" Mary turned to Kiki and bellowed at her, "If you take just *one* of those pills, you'll be addicted! Immediately! And the government puts them out like that! What if any child—"

"We know, Mom!" Mick whispered. "They're just a deterrent! Jesus!"

"Don't swear. Did you know they're used for murder too?"

"Yes, Mom, I watch movies," answered Mick.

"Which movies?" asked Mac-Daddy, frowning at him. "C'mon, everyone. Let's get back to the car. Now." The family hurried away as Mother continued her rant while pushing Kiki's wheelchair:

"Many, many, many times," she scolded Mick too loudly, "in anger, instead of shooting someone, people just knock someone out cold and then shove five or ten opioids down their throats! Get away with murder!"

"I would never do that to anyone, Mom," said Kiki, looking up at Mary-Mac as she rolled her down an alley of chic shops and boutiques, now illumined by an unexpected and soundless burst of lightning from above the dome's glass sphere, lighting the black sky fire-engine red with splotches of unhealthy looking gray.

"Just don't get anyone mad or sad with you," Mary told them as they hurried on. "Cuz they'll murder you with pills! Poison! Bejesus! We're no better than the Russians now!"

"Mary, that's enough!" Daddy insisted, ushering them back to the long line of cars at the Cincinnati dome's border gate.

[In truth, Mary was mostly correct in her angered analysis: There was a huge, unreported murder problem in America-United because of gun-and-opioid-homicides. Truly, in 2036 it was dangerous to even get into an argument with someone. With anyone. Because there was a great chance you could end up dead with zero repercussions for your murderer. Outside the Capital Cities, there was literally no police presence other than the occasional, rarely seen, wandering Government Wizard-drone.]

Mother Mac shakily pontificated on as they approached their Hummer. "The main problem in murdering someone with opioids, I heard once from an untoward Russian source while in line for tomato samples, is the simple problem of keeping the pills down because, even when unconscious, the gag-reflex will cause the victim to continuously try to vomit the pills. The trick is (and this bit of info is straight from a Christian-Family podcast), you have to keep knocking them unconscious when they try to vomit the pills out. You have to just keep beating and beating them in the head, and then the gag-reflex will finally abate."

"Gross, Mom," mumbled Kiki as Mick helped her in the car.

"Well. It's time you learn," Mother-Mary told her sternly.

"Mom, don't get in more trouble," pleaded Mick. "We should leave."

"...And you should always use a pillowcase filled with either oranges or potatoes so there will be no bruising or evidence of murder," remembered Mary-Mac, climbing into the driver's seat.

"You planning on doing something to Dad?" Mick fake-joked with a forced smile upwards at a streetlight Facecam.

"Not yet," quipped Mary back at her first-born twin while the rest of the 'Cuddy-Clan slammed their car doors, waking up Alice in the process.

In fact, Mother Mary speaking her angry words out loud in public did eventually lead to them being singled out and taken in by authorities that day, because sure enough, a Cincinnati citizen reported a "long-haired, wild, Welsh woman raving on the streets," immediately garnering the attention of the Cincinnati border patrol who, if they hadn't before, had definitely noticed Mother Mary McCreedy McGillicuddy by then. Strike One. At present, the fugitive family was in their car with the indicator glowing blood-red on their dash, announcing to Facebook and the world that *here sat a traitor. A dissenter.* An enemy of the ~~TXXXP~~ Regime, who'd committed a crime punishable by death.

And now, strangely enough (as if things couldn't have gotten worse), it looked as if one of the most famous men in the world, United America's Secretary of Defense, Admiral Grayson Bilge, was not only in view on the gold-lined cobblestoned-street in front of them, but was now approaching their car and pointing at them.

Hamilton, Ohio Sticks, December 31, 2036

O ver the last week, fierce fighting had finally spilled down below the Canadian-American border and on into Michigan, then further down, all the way into Southern Ohio. Just north of Cincy was a massive, heavily guarded Goliath of a building, smack-dab on the center of Main Street, in what remained of a town called Hamilton, Ohio (coincidentally, The Cantras had now fought 'from Hamilton to shining Hamilton').

Within this cavernous warehouse was ~~TXXXP~~'s secret stockpile of rare earths.

And now, after seemingly unending vicious battling by the Cantras, it was theirs.

The Cantras had undeniably been kicking ass and taking names, but it was the reconnaissance work that won the day for them in Ohio. J and his army of badasses snuck in early and severed all means of communication by cutting off cellular towers and cables. Ted and Bob had created a giant magnetic field that shut down anything electric within forty square miles; they had painstakingly constructed a machine roughly the size of a house, which was transported on a covered semi-truck. It was all designed well, and everything had proceeded almost too perfectly, practically to the letter, and that's what worried J. Bob and Ted had vamoosed by now, who knows where, amid rumors that the World had only days left of existence (which the pair vehemently insisted was real-truth true).

J couldn't think that way, though. He had to continue fighting. For the future of the human race.

While small battles surged on stubbornly around them in Dayton and Blue Ash, J and his marauders nursed their wounds and plotted in the weeds on the gutted and abandoned grounds of the Hamilton Miami University campus. The Cantras were presently trying to tolerate or at least put up with their American compatriots from the Canadian-American Nonconformist Network Of Terrorists, or the CANNOTs (T̶X̶X̶X̶P̶ had definitely made fun of their acronym like He did the Cantras, recently calling them the "Can't-ras." Even as a cryogenically reanimated head, T̶X̶X̶X̶P̶'s chirpees still had the same sophomoric, biting edge to them).

However, while the Cantras and the CANNOTs had worked together for the Common Good for years now, rarely was it actually *side by side like this*, fighting right next to one another and seizing territories together. And now they were remembering why it was, up 'til now, that the Cantras and the CANNOTs fought their battles separately: The Americans were borderline unbearable, obnoxious boors, including being obsessed with *"names."* Everything was names! Always Jack Blabla did this, and Mary-Lou Beepbeep did that. This was very off-putting to the former Canadians, who had sworn off names and egos and that kind of thing years ago when everything they had ever known was taken from them.

On this day, while J's Marauders were endeavoring to blow up a bridge, a loud American man with long, gray hair (who seemed way too energetic for a ninety-year-old) named General Kenny was dominating the conversation, and the Canadians had had just about enough of him by now.

"Superstars from every country have banded together, man, and saved the world, my brothers and sisters!" General Kenny droned on, preaching through an old-man's drugged-out smile to J's irritated masses. "Throughout time, the true power of celebrities has been argued over, vehemently," Kenny ranted on, "and the currently held belief is that famous and successful people are, and always will be, better than everyone else! It's true! Celebrities are better! It's actually real-life, truly-true! Because it's like, in a way, they were already chosen by the masses, right?! Throughout the history of man, my sweet-babyfaces, the most charismatic and popular of the tribe has always been chosen as the best leaders, and for good reason: Because they are. The best. Maybe not at fighting, or physical strength, per se, but at *leading. Look at* T̶X̶X̶X̶P̶!

He was a celebrity, man! This is the age of celebrities!"

"And look where it's got us," J told him flatly.

"Would you just shut his face?" pleaded an annoyed Cantra soldier, now just finishing the bridge's wiring job. "We've got to do this. Now! OK?"

"Do it," J told him.

"—OK, everyone, fire in the hole. In 3... 2...1."

Everyone huddled low as the Cantra soldier plunged a louver down, and the bridge beside them *exploded in a furious fire cloud* and tumbled to the ground.

"That'll keep the Regime from breathing down our necks from the north..." said J, standing up without fear for his own safety despite the bridge's still-falling remains, "but we've still got the rest of United-America attacking us from the south."

"That's why stealth is still our best weapon, brother!" yelled the ugly American, General Kenny. "As long as our shit stays out of RAMFOX News, we don't exist, man! *We just gotta stay quiet.*"

"Ironic, you talking about being quiet," said RR.

"Ah ha, that's funny, dude. Did you know the leader of practically every rebel army is a former celebrity?! Selena Gomez is leading the biggest army out of the west. A buncha athletes led by Mike Trout's 20,000-strong Death-Patrol is coming from Texas. Over in Illinois and Kentucky, Vince Vaughn's actor-kid along with old rocker-Billy Corrigan's Pumpkin-Legions have amassed to take the Illinois Rare Metals reserves..."

"So what's your point?" blurted RR, beyond irritated by now. "Jesus!"

"I thought all the celebrities were purged at Miller-Time," said a teenaged CANNOT girl.

"Well, that's mostly true," said Kenny. "But a few of us got away."

"Us?" asked J.

"Yeah," said General Kenny, smiling wide, "I used to be a celebrity. Kenny Loggins is my name. And rockin' was my game."

"Oh, yeah. I think I heard of you," muttered J, "back when I was a kid," to which Kenny suddenly stood and began gyrating his old man body and singing inexplicably and gutturally:

"I'm Alright! Nobody worry bout me! I'm Alright! ...Or how 'bout this one: You gotta cut loose! Footloose! Kick off your—"

"—Yeah, I think I remember that one," said nineteen-year-old QT, politely.

"Yeah, that was a good one," reminisced Kenny Loggins, on his game, and at his best now, taking a big celebratory swig of whiskey (because ever since Generals J and Kenny had in tandem taken the strongholds of Michigan and Northern Ohio earlier, smiling together while gazing into the fire of the burning, abandoned T̶X̶X̶X̶P̶ Tower in Columbus, things had been going well for Kenny). "Yeah, that old purge didn't get me," said Kenny Loggins, grinning now at a beautifully blazing bridge.

Kenny was one of very few celebrities who got away. During the fourth Freedom Purge of 2029, by far the biggest, both Jared Kushner and many other Jews (along with any of the remaining left-leaning entertainment industry, including celebrities) were disappeared. Less tragic but also around that time, practically all of the Lyin'-Left-movies were destroyed, which was basically all of the films that ever were (80-something percent of them). America had long ago lost its mantle as film colossus of the world since California had now been gone-and-punished for practically a decade.

In 2036, all movies made in American-United were set in the south-east quadrant with titles like *The Dukes of Hazzard 3, Goin' Screwballs!*, with all Southern white actors. In a way, it was a good thing that America was no longer the arts or entertainment leader of the world. For one thing, China was no longer stealing America's intellectual property, since no one wanted it anymore. Most of the good films nowadays were out of Russia and Russope, and their principal language was Russian with very stilted English subtitles.

Kenny had been speaking at length and ad nauseam for weeks about the power of celebrity... but the more he drank, the older he seemed, and recently, the man had been nipping off his flask frequently. Now gazing drunkenly into the bridge inferno, General-K was spouting more typical old person's misinformation: "Those climate-change-deniers were right all-along," Kenny bloviated. "It was *not* man-made. It was God cleansing the earth of its sinners."

"OK. Please, eh?" a Canadian soldier cut in. "What the hell, eh? Somebody turn him off? He's not even a proper liberal?"

"It's even in our *name*, for cripe's sake!" Kenny said, laughing. "Liberals? What does that even *mean*, like, 'a lot' or 'almost too much'? Like on the shampoo bottle when it says, 'Apply liberally'? 'Liberally'? Are we all 'a lot' or 'almost too much' for people?"

QT smiled and said, "Define liberally.'" Then her phone spoke:

"'lib(ə)rəlē/ adverb
1.
in large or generous amounts:
"she quotes liberally from the Bible"
2.
in a way that is not precise or strictly literal; loosely:
"the law is interpreted liberally"
3.
in a way that involves broadening a person's general knowledge and experience:
"liberally educated students"
4.
in a way that favors individual liberty and moderate political and social reform:
"I used to think more liberally""

"None of that sounds bad to me," said QT, shrugging. "Why *is* 'Liberal' such a dirty word?"

"Naw, we're all 'in large amounts' or whatever you said," argued Kenny. "'Not precise or literal.' That's us."

"'Broadening a person's knowledge,'" QT read off her phone, "...and favoring 'individual liberty and moderate political and social reform.' Well fucking just sue us."

"If you don't like the Liberals, then why are you fighting with us?" RR asked the inebriated General Kenny.

Kenny Loggins scoffed. "Shit, they're better than this Administration. *They* sure fucked things up for *everyone*, that's for sure." The silence signaled that General Kenny had finally said something on which everybody could agree.

Kenny had been looking long and hard at J. Suddenly, he gasped and turned to THC. "Wait a minute. Do you know who that is? *I remember him.*"

"Don't say it."

"Wait a minute, is he....?"

"Don't say it. I mean it."

"Excuse me," said Kenny, softly tapping J on the arm, "but I've just got to ask..."

"Don't," warned J.

...yet Kenny just had to: "Look, sorry, but I have to know. Are you... Justin Bieber?"

J looked down at the ground, his ears growing red in anger.

"Jesus," swore THC.

"Hey!" RR yelled. "No names!"

"I'm alright," said J. "Don't worry about me. Just don't let it happen again." Then J went and quietly brooded (but in a cool way) in the shadows of the dust-forest like a disappearing comet or a superstar.

"Yep. Just Justin and me and the celebs. We are definitely in the process of successfully taking back this world," Kenny Loggins jabbered on, "Just watch, my brothers and sisters."

Two miles beneath the Washington DC White House

December 31, 2036

I t had finally been decided that it was time for the ~~TXXXPS~~ to step down.

And as soon as the nuclear codes were entered, and there was no turning back, at that *very* moment, it became a foregone conclusion. So they were literally stepping down, *way* down, close to three miles into the Earth's crust.

At present, they had been stepping down miles of winding concrete steps for forty-two long minutes, which would eventually lead them to a bunker reserved *exclusively* for an Elite thirty human beings:

The DC White House Bunker Attendees

From the Administration who *weren't* born of the immediate, blood-pure ~~TXXXP~~ family, only three made it:

1. Steven MNUXXXX. By himself. None of the wives or mistresses (he paid multi-quadrillions).

2. Mike PENXX, who was now beginning his first term as the "Failed, nuclear-fallout-era Prez.". Alone. No family permitted (So the white puma could finally roam free, if you catch the drift).

3. KellyaXXX CXXXXY because of loyalty. -- For cripe's sake, she even disappeared her own *husband* for Continued and Habitual Treason, and now *his head was impaled on a pike in Dallas!* That was loyalty.

There were also fourteen celebrities/and/or/others:

Three young celebrity females, all absolute smokin'-hottie actress/singers who were the current flavors-of-the-month (or year), all of them unknown a decade prior, most likely because they were eight years old.

Three similarly attractive men, one from the soap Princess Ivanka followed, and then two old men: Brad Pitt and Ryan Gosling (and decidedly *not* Shawn Mendes, who was in the doghouse "...for many, many reasons that he knows *very well*.").

Four "eggheads," all in their twenties and thirties, ranging in hotness from 7 to 9 (impressive really, when you think about it, because these were all A+++ Triple-Bonafide-Genius-types), including a physician (math) who was also a licensed physician (medical doctor), and an engineer (math) who was also a trained transportation engineer (i.e., he could actually perform as a real, old-timey-engineer and *drive the* trains over the webs of tracks, through the underground snaking tunnels, spider-webbing multi-directionally from their subterranean central bunker, and in one case slithering along almost 250 miles... but leading ultimately to what? What world would be left above? What life forms? The engineer-engineer would be one of the first to find out).

...And then four more were allowed into the bunker who were unofficially known as the "Favors." While it can't be real-fact-factually proven, all evidence shows that these were the chosen members of the three families who coughed up the most dough. Vsgillions upon nonillions upon versillions-worth of old-timey, early-2000s dollars were what had to be ponied up for a pass to the bunker. The actual number in 2036 dollars was astronomical (the dollar's value had been plummeting even *more* recently because, well, what the hell, the world was ending, so the window to cash in had been rapidly closing if not already shut) since the 2036 dollar versus the old 2020 dollar was now at a ratio of about 1-45,000. There was actually no number in existence that could describe the amount these people paid to get a family member in the bunker. The number was beyond mathematical grasp. It has been argued that it was actually closer to the concept of infinity because the contracts they signed stipulated that they would all somehow *keep* paying whatever profits could be made, in any way imaginable, into the protected computer coffers of the ~~TXXXP~~

Family even after the destruction of ALOE (All Life On Earth). This was confusing to most since the concept of infinity wasn't actually a real mathematical thing ("...otherwise the stars would have collapsed in on themselves long ago," said Stephen Hawking once), especially nowadays, when a devastating sense of finite dread permeated everyone constantly. Suffice to say, the Buffet-Gates family, the KXCH family and the BinJal Aminda-al family paid dearly with everything they had ever owned to have their choices live on in the Elite bunker:

Little Jxxxxn Buffet-Gates was the most youthful "Favor" (and the youngest member of anyone chosen for the bunker) at four years old.

Her sister, Rxxxxxe Buffet-Gates, was twelve, and she also got to go.

The *other* two Elite Membership Families ultimately couldn't decide on a younger family member, so two old, white, male heads-in-jars joined the Legion of thirty;

...an eighty-four-year-old figurehead from Dubai (just his head, not his figure) named Geed BinJal Aminda-al

...and the cryogenically frozen head of David KXCH, now 108 years young and dead since 2019, both of them arguably disproving the theory that you can't take it with you.

And lastly, the ~~TXXXP~~-family tallied a grand total of thirteen of the remaining available spots in the best bunker on the planet:

There was, of course, the head of The Family: the actual head of DXXXXD X. ~~TXXXP~~,

...and, naturally, Princess Ivanka ~~TXXXP~~,

Duke-Don ~~TXXXP~~ Jr. II the Younger,

Prince Erikkk ~~TXXXP~~ (He recently had his Christian name legally changed to three K's after Duke-Don II bet Him quadrillions that he wouldn't. Duke-Don II added the hyphen and the II to his royalty name because he thought it was "important and cool."),

...and lastly, Baron Barron ~~TXXXP~~.

In addition, each pure-blood ~~TXXXP~~ received the option to choose up to two of their own children, but since Prince Erikkk chose to barter his kids' choices for the best room in the bunker, those children (all between the ages of nine and sixteen) turned out to be:

XXX ~~TXXXP~~,

XXXX ~~TXXXP~~, and

XXXXX-XXX ~~TXXXP~~ (three females), along with

XXXXXXX ~~TXXXP~~,

XXX ~~TXXXP~~, XXXX ~~TXXXP~~, and

XXX-XXXXXX ~~TXXXP~~ (four males), which brought the grand total in the bunker to thirty.

END OF LIST

Unfortunately, His Eminence's daughter Tiffany, along with the rest of the non-accessory ~~TXXXP~~S not chosen, had to gut it out with the rest of the Losers "Up on the Crust" (the phrase most likely to overtake "Out on the Tiles" as the go-to description of the general, post-holocaust Earth-Wasteland). But that's just the way things go. When you're not a Winner.

The extraordinary bunker to which the Elite Thirty caravan was making its downward pilgrimage was designed with the capacity to rebuild all of human civilization in mind. It was very, very spacious. But still, very, very underground. They had to remain sane, these Chosen Thirty people who might be the next Adam and Eve, or Cain and Abel, or King Davids of the future human race (and think about it: You got four young, hottie ladies in their twenties if you count one of the science chicks... and you had an insatiable cougar in the Princess, who still had active eggs... and tons of eligible (white) guys... so...).

Switching focus to a political lens (and to thankfully change the subject), it was now Mike PENXX's turn to take over. As *soon* as the decision to launch the bombs was made [and the actual, automated launch time was *presently only minutes away*], it was resolved by chirpee that "...the Great Leader Donald ~~TXXXP~~ will officially step down so that the damage is not perpetrated during his actual tenure."

So earlier that afternoon, after the live cameras captured DXXXXD X. ~~TXXXP~~'s head-in-a-jar descending, alone, down the escalator in Saint Louis' premiere mall, Mike PENXX was sworn in on the mall floor in an impressive ceremony, painstakingly made to look and be absolutely real to the public.

Unfortunately, it was safe to say PENXX had inherited a mess. To his credit though, he had really, *really* waited a long time for this chance, in sort of a stoic, nonplussed, pious euphoria (strangely though, even as the *new President, still* no one seemed to notice Mike PENXX on the stairs during the giant, descending journey down). Sure, PENXX was eighty-seven, but it was, *finally,* "*his time.*" Not Miller-Time's. And not the Duke's or the Prince's. It was *PENXX-Time, his* turn to rule the soon-to-be-radiation-poisoned country-with-the-indefinite-name from three miles underground.

So, as the party of thirty continued down, descending the seemingly endless stairway, little four-year-old Jxxxxn Buffet-Gates was the one who did most of the talking.

"Where are we going?"

"I've told you a dozen times," said her sister, holding her hand securely. "We're going to live in an underground hotel. All your stuff's down there already. Don't worry."

"But why?"

"Why what?"

"Why are we going down?"

"Because the Earth is dangerous now. And no one can survive like that, so we're going to a carnival downstairs until it gets better."

"How?"

"It'll just sort itself out, like it always has."

"How?"

"Oh. Just. Nature. It always has a way of having the final say."

"Nature?"

"Yes."

"Why?"

"Because it's much stronger than us."

"Why?"

"Hey," said Duke-Don the Younger, "could we all just have a little silence? Please? I mean our dad just stepped down. This is a tragic day!"

"Totally," muttered Princess Ivanka in agreement, "and don't wake up Daddy, please! He's in his box, in sleep mode, and I'd like to keep Him that way."

"She's just asking," said Jxxxxn's sister. "Sorry."

"No, it's fine," said Princess I. "Just maybe not so much with the political-type issues?"

"She's only four. She doesn't even know what politics is."

"I know," sighed the Princess. "Just. Enough with the gotcha questions, yeah?"

"Sorry..."

"Who's that?" asked Jxxxxn.

"She's a Princess."

"Why?"

"Because She was born that way."

"How?"

"Because Her family is Royalty. The T̶X̶X̶X̶P̶ Family."

"But you said—"

"No, you're mistaken—"

"You said the T̶X̶X̶X̶P̶ family—"

"No, I didn't! You're mistaken!"

"You said—"

"Hey, let her answer," Barron, the superstar heart-throb singing sensation cut in. "The ~~TXXXPS~~ are what...? What did she tell you about the ~~TXXXPS~~, little girl?"

"That they dumb. And mean."

"Wow!" Barron laughed. "That was awesome!"

"You're thinking of someone else, Jxxxxn, that was a family named the Jumps," explained her older sister. "They're totally different from the ~~TXXXPS~~. The ~~TXXXPS~~ are royalty. They are the America-United Royal Family."

"Why?"

"Because They were born that way. And also, God decided it."

"God?"

"God wanted Them to be kings because He thought They were best. The best of people."

"Why is Earth bad now? Why can't they breathe now?"

"Because of bad people. Not any of us. Others."

"Who?"

"Just... Anyone who didn't agree with us. With what we all wanted."

"AKA the Losers," piped in KellyaXXX-CXXXXY. "That's who. Look who won. The Winners. Look who lost. The Losers. End of story."

"What was the prize?" asked the naïve four-year-old.

"For what?" asked KellyaXXX.

"For winning."

"This," answered KellyaXXX with almost no smirk at all.

"You're a lady."

"Yes, I am," KellyaXXX agreed while shooting a quick professional smile at the irritating girl.

"I'm a girl."

"Yes, you are!"

"There not many girls here."

"No, there aren't."

"Good God! It's so fucking loud and echoey and shrill in here," complained the Duke. "Why aren't we taking an elevator?"

"There is no elevator, and it wouldn't function anyway, in the event of a WEE," remarked four-star General Charon, who was accompanying them down. "This is the only way down, as specified."

"Well, can we have some music in here or something?"

"No, sir," answered the General from the front of the line. "There is no signal in here. There will be WiFi in the bunker, but on the two-mile stair, in this chamber, there is no signal, and any device you activate will be scrambled. It's this way purposely. So no one can get to you. No one can attack."

"General!" said Prince Erikkk, taken aback. "There is a small, little girl, right here, and other little children, here, in this place, now!"

"Sorry, sir."

"Am I really a 'sir'?" spat the Prince.

The General sighed a little as he continued his descent down with them. "No, my Prince."

"Dude, is now the time for that?" asked Ivanka's ten-year-old son, XXXXX.

"Whenever," Prince Erikkk snarled back.

"Why are there no girls?" asked little Jxxxxn.

KellyaXXX did a double-take at the four-year-old toddler. "Who me? Uh, because that's just the way the chips fell. To the men. Again."

"Are you power? Lady? Power Lady with. Full."

"A powerful lady?" KellyaXXX asked, helping her out. "Yes, I suppose I am."

"Then why are there no girls? There's only only one, two,

three..."

"Hey, we're over here!" called singer/model Tiffany-Ashley SXXXXXXE from the very back of the descending swarm.

"Yoo-hoo!" and "Hello! Back here!" called Taylor SXXXT's nineteen-year-old starlet daughter, CXXK, and Amber-Tiffanie BXXXM waving frantically on the stairs beside her.

"Yeah, that's the problem!" Duke-Don II cackled, "You're back *there*!"

"Right on, bro," crowed Erikkk, grinning and hi-fiving the Duke, "Like so we could be watching their ASSES, *right!?*"

"Yeah, dude. I think that was the just of the joke, wasn't it? The just of the joke. Wasn't it?"

"Damn. Mellow," mumbled the Prince.

"Maybe also, most of the mean men *already had* the Power," KellyaXXX continued on a little too loudly and pointedly after taking a quick swig from a gold flask, "And the mean men didn't want to give any of the power to the ladies."

"We *really can't have music in here? To drown out the girls? Something?*"

"Sorry, Duke Donald," said General Charon.

"The title is not just 'Duke Donald' by itself. It's just either 'The Duke,' like John Wayne, or 'Duke-Donald ~~TXXXP~~ Jr. The Second, The Younger.'"

"Why not Donald-Duke?" cackled Erikkk. "Like Donald Duck!"

"Ha ha. Shut up, Prince Eric the Red," Don Jr. II shot back.

"Who's that?" asked Erikkk.

The Duke shrugged. "A guy."

"Eric the Red was an explorer, actually," Steve MNUXXXX cut in, grinning widely in a suit and tie as he descended down, slightly above them on the stairs. "I believe he founded Greenland, which was eventually our fifty-third state."

"He said 'founded,'" said the Prince, giggling to the Duke II, then looking back at MNUXXXX. "The word is 'found.' What are you, an infant?"

"Where's Greenland?" asked four-year-old Jxxxxn.

Everyone on the stairs laughed. "Oh, that's been gone for a while now, honey," said Jxxxxn's sister.

"Eric the Red's son," MNUXXXX went on, "was Leif Erikson (c. 970 – c. 1020), the Norse explorer from Iceland."

Princess I., glancing back, was reassured to see that MNUXXXX was reading all this from his phone. "Thank God," she mumbled breathily, "No fracking-rutting-way he would have just 'known' all that without his phone."

"What's this about a phone?" called the General from below, concentrating on the winding stairs beneath him. "No phones!"

"Where's Iceland?" asked the four-year-old.

Everyone laughed at her again, maybe even a little harder this time. Kids.

"Leif Ericson was the first-known European to set foot on continental North America, even before Christopher Columbus!" MNUXXXX exclaimed. "See? Everyone's always saying all this apocalypse-holocaust stuff is our doing! Maybe it was this guy's: Leif Ericson! He was the first WASP to set foot in America! Before Columbus! This is all *his* goddam fault!"

There was a stony silence in the clammy, cavernous staircase chamber as everyone descended further down, so MNUXXXX read on: "According to the Sagas of Icelanders, he established a Norse settlement in former-day Canada. There's a picture of his statue in Minnesota."

"Remind me why we care again?" quipped 'Baron-Squared' (his nickname, thoroughly copyrighted, and also the title of his third album).

"Can I see?" asked little Jxxxxn, reaching back dangerously as the strong hand of her sister suspended her up in the air so she wouldn't topple twenty-two yards to the next landing. (There were over 480 landings before you hit bottom. But the bunker-pack had been descending for close to an hour by now. They were almost there.)

"Hey, is that girl looking at a phone?" asked the General, staring up at them in disbelief.

"Yes," sighed MNUXXXX.

"And how is that digital content not scrambled in the *stair-chamber*?!" asked General Charon pointedly to his military assistant.

"Oh, please..." sneered MNUXXXX from the middle of the descending swarm and rolling his eyes.

"Seriously, *how is that phone working*?" demanded the General.

"Your system 'works,' General, don't worry," MNUXXXX explained, speaking down to him. "I know people. I had my phone augmented. Big whoop."

"But there are supposed to be no redundancies, Lieutenant!" the General snapped accusingly at his blushing, uniformed assistant.

"Please, you child," the sardonic seventy-three-year-old MNUXXXX told the sixty-nine-year-old General, "There's nothing money can't buy. Don't you know that by now?"

There was a long, stony silence. "Yes, sir, yes I guess I do," answered the General softly.

Another silence loomed over them (soundless other than their continuous, echoing footsteps), which was broken again by the four-year-old girl: "Are the army men staying at the hotel with us too?"

Everyone laughed. "Good ice-breaker!" the Duke laughed. "Thank God for children sometimes, right? I mean sometimes? Right?" Everyone silently agreed with small, tight smiles.

"No, darling," said the General warmly, looking up to little Jxxxxn. "The army men have to stay here on the stairs, and up above too. Remember all those doors we passed on the way down the stairs? That's where we're going to live. The army men."

"Why?"

"Well, to make sure you're safe."

"From what?"

"Justin Bieber's Marauders," muttered the Princess.

"Ivanka, please! The kids!" Prince Erikkk reminded her, gob-smacked.

"What's a rauder?"

"We're going to make sure you're all safe down here so you can be President someday, little girl!" said the General, smiling.

At this, KellyaXXX snorted so hard in a sudden burst of laughter that actual snot came out and sprayed the nape of the Duke's neck with a fine mist. "Gross! Kelly!"

"Sorry. Oh my God, I'm so sorry, Duke-Don," she said, mortified.

"But it *was* hilarious," purred Ivanka, smiling as She descended down past some of the lowest places left in the world.

"What is these floors?"

"They're called landings. —How many more landings left?" asked Jxxxxn's sister.

"Less than thirty now," said General Charon, smiling up at her reassuringly from his position below.

"Less than thirty! Yay!" said one of the eggheads.

"What's a landing?"

"It's those little floors along the stairs."

"That's why they're called landings," mused Ivanka. "Because if you fell and didn't land on the landing, you'd never stop falling and never land."

"...Ever," added Steve MNUXXXX.

"We can fall to neverland?" asked the little girl.

"Sure, I suppose," said Princess I., rolling her eyes.

"I like this picture," said the little girl, looking into the smart-phone as everyone continued descending into the ground.

"Let me see," said the Duke II, taking the phone away. This is what he saw:

◆ ◆ ◆

2015
Statue of Leif Erikson in St. Paul, Minnesota, United States

Born c. 970 Icelandic Commonwealth
Died: c. 1020 Greenland
Nationality: Norse: Icelandic–Norwegian
Occupation: Explorer
Known for: First European in North America;
Partner(s)

Thorgunna (c. 999)
Children:
Thorgils
Relatives: Erik the Red (father), Þjóðhildur (mother), Thorvald, Thorstein and Freydís (siblings).
Leif was the son of Erik the Red, the founder of the first Norse settlement in Greenland and of Thjodhild (Þjóðhildur).

◆ ◆ ◆

"*Whatever*," said Duke-Don, handing it behind him to Kelly-aXXX, who glanced at it quickly.

"Oh, how sweet," KellyaXXX cooed with bored eyes. "Leif Ericson had only had one partner, Thorgunna, born in the year 999."

"That's what we're gonna start calling you now. Thorgunna," said Prince Erikkk, receiving a loud guffaw and a lo-five from his bro.

"OK, I guess I'll take that," said KellyaXXX, before calling down to the General who had just disappeared below the next landing area. "Can we rest? General? For a minute?"

"Only a few more minutes, ma'am," came his voice.

"Yeah, I know, but please? I feel sick."

General Charon peeped up over the landing floor and then called out up the stairs: "Everybody have a seat! Let's rest for a few." There were twenty-odd grunts as everybody sat down on whatever step or landing they were on. KellyaXXX sat by Jxxxxn, who continued relentlessly questioning her (this was the age, after all, when they did that).

"Why are the men mean?"

"What's that, honey?" KellyaXXX asked the little girl. "The men who are mean? *Why* are they mean? I don't know. I guess because they know for absolute sure that they're right, and theirs is the only way. They believe it so much that they'd even fight you over it and risk everything to win. They would even bet every-one's *else's* life on it."

"Why don't they just be nice?"

"What's that, honey?" asked KellyaXXX.

"The Golden Rule."

"What's that, honey? You mean 'Silence is Golden'? Cuz you haven't learned that one very well yet."

"No. The Golden Rule," explained the little one's sister for her. "Do unto others as you would have them do unto you."

"It means to be nice to others," explained the toddler.

"That's nice," said KellyaXXX with a faraway smile.

"It fixes everything."

"It really does," insisted her older sister. "It's the truth. It's the answer to everything in life."

"My, what a funny little cult you two must have grown up in," KellyaXXX said, smiling down at them.

"What's this about?" asked one of the eggheads, the physician physician, descending a bit lower to listen.

Jxxxxn's older sister recapped: "We're saying if everyone who lived had just been nice to one another, then everything would have been solved, and no bad stuff would have ever happened."

MNUXXXX smirked. "Cute."

"No, it's true," Jxxxxn's twelve-year-old sister insisted again, her eyes clear and confident. "If, before today, *every single person* had started doing *all the right things, together*, and they did that for a few months, or even just *weeks, or days*, the Earth would never have been allowed to die. Because then no one could ever have purposefully hurt anyone anymore. So all this time, before now, we *could have* made it perfect, if every decision had been carried out with kindness, not based on ego, but based on helping out the human species. If every person everywhere—"

"Exactly!" exclaimed MNUXXXX testily, "But you can't get everyone, everywhere, to all do the same thing! The world is too damned big!"

"Maybe it *was* too big. And stupid. But as of tomorrow, it will be much smaller. And smarter."

Everyone looked up at the speaker. It was the cosmologist egghead who had joined the discussion now. "I deign to beg your pardon?" asked Erikkk up to him, condescendingly.

"Just say it's true, that it was impossible to get every person on a planet of billions to make every decision a kind and decent one. Well... Now we *can* do it. We have the *will* because our world is gone. And we have the *way*, because the little girl's sister is right. It's doable, and it would have actually solved *everything*."

"And how does this work?" asked Ryan Gosling sexily, leaning back with his arms crossed.

"Simple," said the cosmologist. "If everybody is always just 'nice' to each other, and really tries to 'help' everyone else, then we survive as a race. That's it."

"And this would work because...?" prompted MNUXXXX impatiently.

"OK. Let's say, for example, you have quadrillions of dollars."

"Not anymore..." MNUXXXX mourned.

"Well, currently money has no purpose until the world gets back on its feet in a few years, but what if, in the old days, you and the other trillionaires had given away half of your money. Since you couldn't possibly have spent it all anyway."

"Given it to what?" asked David KXCH's head in a jar.

"Let's say to schools. Then everybody would have been educated and not fooled into believing lies and worshipping false Gods."

"Hey, watch it," warned Duke-II.

"That's absolutely fake news!" MNUXXXX protested.

"...Or say you gave it away to help with healthcare for all, free of corruption and self-gain. Then we all wouldn't have separated into haves and have-nots where you have to be rich to get sick. Or say you all gave half your money to build clean energy. Stop the planet's rot. We could have. Back twenty years ago."

"OK, fine," said Sheik Geed BinJal Aminda-al's old, jarred-up head impatiently, "If everyone always 'does the right thing' from now on, then these thirty people, right here, will thrive. Then what?"

"...And before we even *get* to that," another egghead cut in, "can these thirty people even accomplish *that task?*"

"True," said the physician physician. "I see here mostly greedy, old, white men. How are they going to suddenly alter themselves into altruistic beings? Waiting for the old people to die is not a political strategy. But I *also* submit it can't be done anyway, even with these smaller numbers, because clearly it's been proven that humans don't possess the will or instinct to save themselves from extinction anymore, even from self-inflicted harm, and even when we had fifty-plus years to do it. Somewhere along the line, we lost our instinct for survival. It's uncanny, but true. We *knew, yet we didn't act* fifty or thirty or twenty years ago. Because we're cynical. Because we always need "more proof." Humans do. As a rule. Then we conveniently move the bar on what "proof" or reality actually is, anything but face our inconvenient truths. And *then*, even when the final, agreed-upon "proof" is in, we'll *still* procrastinate until the last shred of the worn-out skeleton of the planet is nearly used up, until its very final, physical second... And *then* we'll act."

"...Or at least we'll look back on it and judge," said Brad Pitt. "Like this discussion now, I guess."

The General had been smiling up at them, sitting with his arms crossed, for what had become an uncomfortably long time. Finally, he spoke: "Did you know we found the Lost City of Atlantis? A few years ago? In the Atlantic?"

"What?!/Huh?/What was that?!" asked all the eggheads.

"Absurd!" bellowed MNUXXXX.

"No, it's true. It's why it was originally called the Atlantic

Ocean: Atlantis."

"Then why is the other one called the Pacific?" quizzed Erikkk.

"Because it's... pacifying..." said MNUXXXX, jamming his phone into Erikkk's hands. "Google it. —What do you mean 'you found Atlantis'?"

"Yeah," said General Charon. "It was all broken up, twelve miles down in the dark, dark, dead seas. We decided not to release the information to the public. Not yet. But now it doesn't matter anymore, really. Does it? What we learned was that it actually wasn't some beautiful civilization like people dreamed it was."

MNUXXXX had already snatched back his contraband phone and was reading aloud from it: "In Plato's story, Atlantis wasn't at all 'the perfect society.' They were the opposite; Atlantis was the definition of a materially wealthy, technologically superior, and militarily dominant country that had become corrupted by its own wealth, stubbornness, and need for power. The city's enemy, Athens in the former Greece, watched as Atlantis become a sunken civilization."

"They became savages at the end," said the General, "unable to make a decision that was good for themselves anymore. Much like our modern-day world, I guess. If Atlantis came back today, the Atlanteans would probably just try to either kill or enslave everyone again. So, I guess they *were* just like us. They became first-class assholes. And eventually, they did themselves in." The General shrugged a little, got up, and continued the trek down. "We should go," he said, "We've almost arrived at the bottom."

"So there. The two young girls are factually correct," said the engineer engineer, rising to step down along with the rest. "That should be our plan. It's really the only plan there is. To change. To start from zero. Default setting. And, unlike Atlantis, I guess, learn to do it right this time."

"Starting with this group of cynics?" Ivanka reminded him with a smirk.

"Well, there *will be* other survivors," said a hottie female egghead. "In a few years, there could still be a few thousand humans scattered around the earth. Mutated and radiation-poisoned, yes, but alive. Human life *could go on* outside of our bunker of thirty."

"Maybe even like *zombies maybe?*" asked Erikkk.

"Shh."

"I know of a ship headed to Gliese 667 with a few people on board," added the physician physician.

"What's gleep?" asked Jxxxxn.

"Gliese. It's *supposedly* the closest planet with habitable human conditions," MNUXXXX said, rolling his eyes again. "And it's *twenty lights years away*. Good luck!"

"Well, still, they've got a chance," the egghead physician replied, "Just like we do." The rest of the trip was mostly excited murmuring as the downward journeyers were at last able to see the ground approaching them.

At the bunker door, finally, the General beamed up at his pride of fallen angels. "We're here! We've reached rock-bottom. Nowhere left to go now except into hiding to lick our wounds so we can live to fight another day. Right? No place to go but up."

Jxxxxn and her sister both looked 'up,' searching above for the places they'd just descended from, but they saw nothing. Only darkness.

...or maybe just a glimpse of movement. —What was that anyway?

Then, materializing out of the gloaming above came the flickering glimmer of Stephen MXXXXR's forehead, followed by Stephen MXXXXR himself, along with another man.

"M-Miller-Time?" stammered Don II in awe. "What are you doing here?"

"Is that... *Bruno?*" asked the Princess.

In an instant, Miller-Time and Bruno pulled out Lugers and shot General Charon and his assistant.

The gunshots and screams echoed cacophonous-loud in the

dark chamber as MXXXXR yelled above it: "Really? We don't have room for Miller-Time down here? Try again!"

MXXXXR then aimed and assassinated acting President Mike PENXX whose last and only words were simply, "Ow!!... Jesus-*Christ*...!!" before crumpling to the stairs.

"And seriously?" asked Miller-Time, over the echoing blast. "You gave tickets to a pair of old, severed heads?" With that, Secret Service Agent Bruno shot the heads of old men KXCH and Bin-Jal Aminda-al directly through their respective jars and brains.

"What the hell's going on out there?" asked DXXXXD X. ~~TXXXP~~'s head from inside his box.

"Just go back to sleep, Daddy!" bawled Princess I., shaking on the floor behind Erikkk and completely traumatized.

"Why did those two heads *even count as 'people'*? Same as these guys," added Miller-Time, shooting a male hunk between the eyes. "See, I never even *liked* Shawn Mendes. Why were you preserving *him*?"

"That wasn't Shawn Mendes! It was Geoffrey-Allan Dixxon from *Days of Our Lives*!!" cried Princess Ivanka.

"Oh," said MXXXXR. "Well, still. What I said. *And hey!* Looks like you got room for me and Bruno now! So! Who's got the keys to that bad boy?"

Cincinnati December 31, 2036

The McGillicuddys sat in a gleaming gold detaining cell in The Cincinnati Police Station while Admiral Grayson Bilge paced and studied the sorry family.

"Can I ask again, please," Mother Mary implored him for the third time, "why the sodding Secretary of Defense for the entire United-America is taking such an interest in our stupid little Irish-American family's problems?"

"It's a good question," said Admiral Bilge.

"Ya think?" asked Mary.

"You don't agree with the way things have gone in the world, do you?"

"Ya think?" piped Kiki.

"You are all dissenters, are you not?"

"Obviously we would never admit to such a thing, *ever*, would we?" countered Mac-Daddy in disgust.

"No, I guess not," admitted Bilge.

"Just let *them* go!" begged Mary. "I've said some bad things. Recently. I have. And I'm sorry. I might be going through menopause. I'm on the list to see a woman's doctor in four to six months in North Platte, so that will help. My moods are just all over the place. I'm sorry. But *let my family go!*"

"Yes, well, I'm afraid waiting four months for anything is quite out of the question now. You see, the bombs have already been launched. Everything is over."

The McGillicuddys stared. "I beg your pardon?" asked Mick.

"The world has ended," said Admiral Grayson Bilge. "In less than eighteen minutes, it will all be gone."

This breaking information effectively flummoxed the McGillicuddys, who could only sit in silence, inert, mouths gaping.

Daddy Mac managed the word, "I—" Mick threw up.

"Oh, Mick, for God's sake!" said Mary Mac.

"*Sorry! Jesus*, Mom! *You can't stop nagging me* even when every-one's about to *die*!?"

Daddy-Mac asked: "This is true!?"

"Yes," said the Admiral. "Would you follow me, please?"

"Should I come too?" asked Alice, still hanging around.

"Please," said the Admiral, opening a door leading into a 200-yard-wide, cavernous room with a 200-foot-long rocket-type ve-hicle in the center of it.

"What the bleeding—?"

"Please," repeated Bilge, ushering them toward the spaceship. "We're in a bit of a hurry."

"Let's go, Admiral!" came a voice from inside the ship. The per-son behind the voice walked outside, a man who seemed extraor-dinarily over-tanned.

"This is Dr. Robert Fuller, formerly of NASA," said the Admiral.

"Hi, I'm Bob," said the man. "I'm supposed to drive this mon-strosity."

"Look, Mr. Bilge, Mr. Secretary of War," sputtered Mary, "I think we're all in a state of shock about all of this. I mean, I don't understand why you're even spending this *time* with us to—"

"Because I've chosen your children."

"I beg your pardon?"

"Kiki and Mick. They can go."

"Go where?"

"Away. To live on. To start again. On a different planet. This one's used up. This rocket can fit nine. Amongst others, we have a woman of color named Georgette who we need to preserve, my-self and my son Carroll, and... Well, Kiki and Mick can go."

"Why us?" asked Mick.

"I chose you randomly. I thought it was important. Someone

needs to live on who isn't a rich, old conservative man. Some-body. So I asked the dome patrol if there were any very young Lib-eral dissenters captured today, and they pointed at your car. Said they were about to take you in because your Facebook light had gone red."

"I, I need *more proof,* though!" cried Mother-Mary. "How do we know the Earth is ending?"

"Well, they should be in sight now. I'll just open the roof. —Ready for takeoff?" the Admiral shouted into the ship's open hatch as he punched a button on the wall.

"We're all good," came a voice, followed by another very, very tan man. "T-minus ten minutes! Let's go!"

"This is Dr. Cliff Theodore, who helped plan this with me. Dr. Ted, I'm asking these children to accompany us."

"You going with us?" Dr. Ted asked Kiki and Mick. "Just call me Ted. Or Doc, same diff."

"Dr. Ted, here, has chosen an inconvenient time to tell me he isn't *gay* anymore, and we're no longer an *item*," said Dr. Bob, seething a little, "Nice, huh?"

"It's probably a good thing since we're both obviously going to have to procreate a bit from now on..." Ted reminded him.

"A salient point, I suppose..." said Bob grudgingly.

By now the roof had fully retracted, as well as a fifty-foot square of the glass dome, and, as the rain poured hard into the hangar from the clear, sunny blue skies above, there were doz-ens, maybe hundreds of small shining lights, floating, churning, trailing smoke, and heading towards them. "Those are all nuclear warheads," claimed the Admiral soberly, looking up through the falling rain.

"Jesus," said Ted, blinking into the drops of water and the cold sun, staring up at the spectacle in the sky. "We gotta get outta this place. Let's go, peeps." Dr. Ted disappeared into the ship with Dr. Bob sulking behind him.

"Oh m-my God," stuttered Kiki.

"Yeah, that looks like a takeoff in more like six minutes," called the Admiral. "Start her up!"

The rocket *roared to life* while being pelted, hard, by the odd, sunny rain.

"Sorry," shouted the Admiral, "I know that's loud. What's your decision?"

The McGillicuddy parental units were stymied. This was not a decision that was included in any parenting manual. And they had only a minute to decide. "I'm so sorry!" cried Mother Mary. "But you two should go!"

Kiki and Mick looked at their parents in numb despair.

"I'm so sorry!" shouted Mary-Mac.

"No!" shouted Kiki.

"We're so sorry!" Daddy yelled.

"I love you so much!" blubbered Mary, hugging her children. "I'm so sorry! About everything!"

"We're so sorry!" cried Daddy-Mac.

"Why are you apologizing?" Mick's puberty-encumbered voice shrieked, tears streaming down his face. "What are you sorry about?"

"I don't know!" shouted back Mac-Daddy. "Just everything!"

"We're so *sorry*!" Mary repeated.

"About what?!" yelled Kiki.

"About this! That we did this! That we ruined the planet!"

"You didn't ruin the planet!" yelled Mick. "Everyone else did! And you saved us, Mom, *because* you're a dissenter."

"Ha! How 'bout that!" shouted Mary through raindrops and tears.

"Thank you," said Mick.

"Thank you, Mommy," said Kiki, crying.

"Look, there's no time!" said Mary. "We're just *so sorry,* and you need to go now!"

"OK, Mommy," said Kiki.

"We love you so much!" sobbed Mac-Dad, hugging them. "We're so sorry!"

"We're so sorry!"

"We are too!"

"Goodbye!"

"We're sorry!"

"Goodbye!"

"You can go too," the Admiral said to them.

The McGillicuddys turned to the Admiral. "What's that?" shouted Mary.

"You can all go. All of you. I wasn't sure. But now I am. There were no 'amongst others' traveling in the rocket. There was just those four and me. And now I'm not going. I'm a coward because I wanted to go. But I have nothing left to offer. Only more war. Take care of my son, will you?"

"What are you saying?"

"I'm not going," said Bilge, the rain pouring down his face. "Your whole family is. If you want." The Admiral turned to Alice. "There's room for five now. It's going to be cramped, but you can go too. If you want."

Alice laughed at the Liberal Losers. "I ain't goin'. I'm stayin' right here."

"You'll die," said the Admiral, glancing at the incoming. "And frankly, we could use your help in perpetuating the human race."

Alice's eyes grew large. "Are you tellin' me I'm supposed to get-together with those Doctor-Libtards and have babies with 'em or something? No goddam way!"

"No, they have refrigeration and test tubes on board, and all they'd need are your eggs every now and then. Then they'll "hatch" the babies when you all land at your new home. Look at it this way: Maybe you getting on this rocket is the ultimate example of pulling yourself up by your bootstraps. Because if you don't, you'll die here, standing next to me, with no boots left at all. Maybe think of it that way."

"Yeah, maybe... I guess when you put it like that," Alice mused, staring up at the troubled skies. "But just so you know, I've eaten people. A lot."

"Well... maybe just don't do that," suggested the Admiral.

Alice shrugged. "OK."

Dr. Bob hurried out the hatch. "We gotta go! Now!"

"Dr. Bob Fuller, this is Alice. She'll be going with you."

Bob shook hands with her, studying her "outdoorsy" appearance. "Maybe we've *just* got time for you to take a quick shower. For the last time in twenty years? Before we go on this ship? Together?"

"I'm good," said Alice, disappearing into the craft.

"She's a peach..." said Bob.

"You have no idea," Mac-Dad assured him.

"Good luck," Grayson Bilge told them.

"Goodbye, Admiral," Daddy-Mac said as they all clambered in the ship's hatch. "We'll write songs about you in the new land. You'll be like the new planet's George Washington or Johnny Appleseed or Davey Crock—"

Alice's voice came from within: "Aw, just shut up and get on, you fuckin' snowflake-socialist-liberal, fuckin' snowflakes."

"I really want her to be wise or adorable in some way," said Mary, "but she *really is* just an absolute dick, isn't she?"

"Yeah," the Admiral agreed. "It might be a long trip for her, among the only surviving Liberal faction I know of, but you'll all be OK."

The family thanked the Admiral, all of them offering 'Thank yous' and 'I'm sorrys' to each other. Finally, underneath the sky's breathtaking, looping/arching rain of incoming bombs, shining down like water, now only minutes away, the confused and grateful McGillicuddys hurriedly disappeared into the spaceship.

The rocket's red glare was blinding.

J and his marauders perched on top of a large pile of rare earth reserves, having fought their way all the way down past the Kentucky border.

As of this moment, however, they were all merely sitting in the rain and calmly watching the incoming missiles in the sky, wondering what they had been fighting over all this time. They had at last achieved their lofty goal: They possessed and controlled the earth's main rare-earth supply.

For one day. And then the three suicidal, sociopathic dictators of Earth decided in a frenzied rage to turn the Monopoly board over and storm away like none of it ever happened. How does one play with or exist alongside people like that? People who just make up their own rules and break them anytime they want? How does one survive with absolutely no rules?

Evidently, one doesn't.

J stood up on their mountain of rare minerals and looked down at his thousands of rain-soaked people, his head haloed magnificently by the sun and the incoming warheads, which now appeared to be flying through a giant rainbow in the clear blue skies.

J smiled, and that sparkle of old showed in his eyes.

Then, at that moment, for the first time in decades, he sang the simple strains of his biggest hit song from the distant past:

"Sor-ry!"

His followers all silently looked up at him, like the calm before the storm...

...Then they all sang it together: "Sorr/Sorr/-y/y/y/y..."

Over this, QT and Z began loudly rapping the big current

smash-hit, "Burst" by J and the Marauders featuring THC, RR, KIM3, D-D, NTN, NME, FGYF The Creator, DRT, JOU, JOI, U-BO-The-Killer, D2, FR, F2, H99, H2O, NJJV, Killer-J44, JKK and NUM4.

"One man."

"What?"

"Promising things."

J: "*Sor-ry*!!"

"Say what?"

"He promised things to powerful people."

"Powerful people."

"The powerful."

J: "*Sor-ry*!!"

"The Powerful Few."

"You can rule the world."

"You can have all the power."

"But that's not all it takes."

"Not at all/Not at all."

J: "*Sor-ry*!!"

"Hijacked the power."

"Cuz He had the Rare Earths for battle."

"Rare Earth. Celebrate."

"Get Ready, Big Brother."

"Promises of it. To make the weapons."

"Promises of the Power."

J: "*Sor-ry*!!"

"And then anybody, any crime family..."

"...Anyone could do whatever they wanted."

"Whatever He wants."

"Forever."

"Forever."

J: "*Sor-ry!!*"

"Powerful."

"Do whatever they want."

"Forever."

"Yeah. Forever."

"But I know."

"What's that?"

"The key to all happiness."

"Say it."

"You've got to have heart."

("I'm sorry.")

"Don't forget."

("I'm sorry.")

"Never forget."

("I'm sorry.")

"Forever."

J. Bieber continued his guttural belting-out/crooning of "*SORRY!*" to the beat of "Burst," now being chanted in unison by huge swarms of his soldiers (there must have been a million), all singing like it was for the last time in their lives. He even did a few old Justin Bieber moves, spinning on his heels, with his hands in a beating heart-shape.

(THC and RR couldn't be found because they had finally hooked up at the last moment, off to the side (so THC could scratch that particular thing off her bucket-list), and why not? Who's to say what's the proper way to go?)

...And it was beautiful the way they all went down, in the sunny rain like that. Because they died doing what humans ultimately did best—stirring up the crowd as one unit into a fever pitch of celebration and excitement, where no one had to do anything of any consequence except wash in the thrill of what could have been. *This* was what humans did best. [In fact, the music of the human race was by far their biggest contribution to the universe over the long haul of time... So, in effect, after all was said and done, the only material thing of any kind of "worth" on Earth was not the monies or the fuels, it was the art ("Burst" continued to be a big hit for generations, around the universe).]

[To (try to) explain exactly *why* the closing of humanity's final curtain occurred: Basically, the "axis of freedom" had a spat. About what didn't matter. In short, it was typical sanctions, tariffs, posing, and red lines that were dared to be crossed and then were, and thereafter, since nothing else could be thought out to soothe three uncreative old-man-egos, everyone simply launched all their nuclear bombs at each other as they promised they would, all silently wagering they would be disarmed by ~~TXXXP~~-brand Technology's 'Space Force!' in mid-air.

But regrettably, ~~TXXXP~~'s 'Space Force!' turned out to be just like Reagan's 'Star Wars'. Fake propaganda. Another con job.]

Grayson Bilge stood alone in the rain with his wife in the open hangar. He was trying to think zen-like thoughts about how truly sorry he was that his decisions lent a hand to this ending. He looked at her as if for the first time. "God, you're beautiful," Grayson said to her, and she glowed brightly with love as she smiled and took his hand. Then, with their eyes closed, the bombs made contact with Cincinnati. Because the Admiral knew he had to go down with his ship.

And he hoped he was forgiven. By Whatever Else must be out there. In the Beyond.

He hoped there was a Beyond.

The After-Math

Look. Here's the good news:

1. The place was completely trashed, which is fantastic in a clean sweep/good riddance/fresh-start kind of way. After all, how many years were those giant Epcot Center cities going to dodge tsunamis? Another few? Best to start again clean.

2. Another positive thing about all this: The High-Energy nukes didn't kill absolutely everyone. Obviously not. You can't nuke every square inch of a planet. Man and Womankind was still decades away from that kind of technology. There were literally hundreds of humans left alive on earth after the year 2040. ...Well, maybe "many dozens" (*Definitely* dozens)... And the best way to describe the way things were in the new, Post-Nuke "Extremely Low-Energy" era would be to refer yourself to the second of the "Mad Max" movies, 1982's *The Road Warrior* (not the first movie, and definitely not the third because there wasn't anything like a 'thunderdome' or any person remaining who looked remotely like a young Tina Turner or Mel Gibson et al, at all). The survivors left on earth were unfortunately very hideously scarred, radiation-tainted human mutant-types (Sorry!!... trying to keep this positive (!!), ..but after all, it *was* a nuclear holocaust...!). And yes, in Post-World-War-III Earth, mankind continued that whole killing-each-other-over-the-last-remaining-drops-of-oil-that-they-could-squeeze-out-of-the-Earth thing... BUT there was one glaring exception! And it was:

3. The Chinasty (See? More good news!) had always encouraged solar and wind-powered cars, so their post-nuke pirate-marauders were whipping around their con-

tinent like the old *Fast and Furious* films of old (the ones which Dear Leader ~~TXXXP~~ and His Family so loved), driving their death-mobiles all the way until the very end. And those Chinese clans survived for another good, solid twenty or thirty years... so that's some *other* really nice, good news right there.

Ipso facto, after all was said and done, in many ways what happened wasn't so bad, given the choices made by the whole humans-on-Earth-stint from really the beginning of its infancy. And it's at least sort of satisfying to know the *real-true* answer to the Universally asked, proverbial riddle:

"What would **you** do to save your entire species (in this case, Earth-Humans), from extinction if **you** had all of the necessary information which warned **you** about it decades before, with plenty of chances to right the ship?"

Unfortunately, no human particularly likes the real-fact answer to this riddle, but at least it's satisfying to know the (real) truth about what eight billion humans could accomplish: ; (the answer to the riddle is actually sort of a silly, Kaufmanesque non-response, because the true answer is *'nothing'*).

"...And if you feel sad, remember there are comets flying around willy-nilly that *could have* and probably still will annihilate Earth at some time anyway." —That was part of the feel-good message that whoever-the-President-was-then sent out over the WiFi the day after the holocaust. That and to "Remember the old-time wagon trains, also, if you're sad." [Little was ever heard again from the inhabitants of the Presidential bunker. Maybe they're down there still, playing at "ruling."]

So... just don't fret. OK?

However, maybe if **you** all wanted to do something about it now, that would be fantastic too (we're going to try to get all this info into a black hole soon, in effect, sending it back in time to warn you, but we doubt this will change anything that happens, really. Because we are you. And we were there. And we did nothing. And we're *sorry*. And it makes us, just, *mind-bogglingly sad that none of you will do anything*. Believe us, we know, but, *Hey*, we figure we've got to at least *try, right?*)!

Anyway, we are flying now. Bob and Carroll and Ted and Alice, plus a sweet woman named Georgette (who's like a celebrity onboard), along with the family: Mary, Mickey, Mac, and Kiki, and we are *writing this together on a spaceship*, attempting to travel twenty-two light years away to the planet Gliese 667c to start again. (Supposedly though, according to Einstein, *it will only "feel" like six years!* And everybody on-board agrees that's **_great news!_**)

Here are a few thoughts from the crew:

Hi, everyone. The idea is to travel an average of one light-year per Earth-year. Including 512 refueling stops, we'll get there in less than twenty-three Earth years. We'll keep in touch. Love and kisses. —Dr. Ted

I vow to edit this text so that no one will have to read the ~~TXXXP~~'s names, or any of the other human rights violators' and war-criminals' names, and to protect the names of the innocent. —Georgette

That was kind of harsh. —Carroll

Agreed. —Alice

Quiet and drink your Tang. You two are outnumbered here... but *now* in a way where it actually *means something*. —Love and peace. —Mac-Dad

Think we can do it? Start again? —Mick

Think we *should*? —Dr. Bob

Think we even deserve to? —Mary

Yes. —Kiki

P.S.

(For support, one might do well to remember our new mantra, the mantra we will pass down to all Human Life on Gliese)

But I know.

What's that?

The key to all happiness.
Say it.
You've got to have heart.
(I'm sorry)
Don't forget.
(I'm sorry)
Never forget.
(I'm sorry).

The End

"Ozymandias" by Percy Bysshe Shelley

I met a traveller from an antique land
Who said: "Two vast and trunkless legs of stone
Stand in the desert ... Near them, on the sand,
Half sunk, a shattered visage lies, whose frown,
And wrinkled lip, and sneer of cold command,
Tell that its sculptor well those passions read
Which yet survive, stamped on these lifeless things,
The hand that mocked them, and the heart that fed:
And on the pedestal these words appear:
'My name is Ozymandias, king of kings:
Look on my works, ye Mighty, and despair!'
Nothing beside remains. Round the decay
Of that colossal wreck, boundless and bare
The lone and level sands stretch far away.

Thank you so much for reading this book! I'd like to stress how important it is for new authors to get reviews, so I'd thank you to do so, if you feel so inclined, and pleasedo check out my other books. Thanks

Thanks also to Reedsy for all their help, and Margaret Diehl for editing. Also, thanks to my family and neighbors for putting up with me while I wrote this.

◆ ◆ ◆

Michael Sandels is the writer of many novels, plays, screenplays, short stories, and his own stand-up comedy. He received a BA in English from Carleton College in 1986 and an MFA from Temple University in 1989. Hailing from Chicago and LA, Mike now lives in Northern New Jersey with his family of six.

His other novels, *It's the End of the Word as We Know It, artism, Extra Special Sauce, Two Thumbs Sticking Up!, The Water Salesman,* the autobiographical *Portrait of a Young Couple,* and his children's book "The Magical, Grown-Up ABC Phone Book" are available in paperback, digital, and audiobook either now or soon, on Amazon, Kindle, and more.

This is the first novel or novella Mike has ever released (so please leave a good review and tell a friend, gentle reader). Love